Songs for Angel

Songs for Angel

MARIE-CLAIRE BLAIS

Translated by Katia Grubisic

ARACHNIDE

First published as *Des chants pour Angel* in 2017 by by Les Éditions du Boréal
First published in English in 2021 by House of Anansi Press Inc.
www.houseofanansi.com

House of Anansi Press is committed to protecting our natural environment. This book
is made of material from well-managed FSC®-certified forests, recycled materials, and
other controlled sources.

House of Anansi Press is a Global Certified Accessible™ (GCA by Benetech)
publisher. The ebook version of this book meets stringent accessibility standards and
is available to students and readers with print disabilities.

25 24 23 22 21   1 2 3 4 5

Library and Archives Canada Cataloguing in Publication

Title: Songs for Angel / Marie-Claire Blais ; translated by Katia Grubisic.
Other titles: Des chants pour Angel. English
Names: Blais, Marie-Claire, 1939- author. | Grubisic, Katia, translator.
Description: Translation of: Des chants pour Angel.
Identifiers: Canadiana (print) 20200393987 | Canadiana (ebook) 20200399047 |
ISBN 9781487006327 (softcover) | ISBN 9781487006334 (EPUB) | ISBN
9781487006341 (Kindle)
Classification: LCC PS8503.L33 D4713 2021 | DDC C843/.54—dc23

Cover design: Alysia Shewchuk
Text design and typesetting: Lucia Kim

*House of Anansi Press respectfully acknowledges that the land on which we operate
is the Traditional Territory of many Nations, including the Anishinabeg, the Wendat,
and the Haudenosaunee. It is also the Treaty Lands of the Mississaugas of the Credit.*

 Canada Council
for the Arts

Conseil des Arts
du Canada

 ONTARIO ARTS COUNCIL
CONSEIL DES ARTS DE L'ONTARIO
an Ontario government agency
un organisme du gouvernement de l'Ontario

With the participation of the Government of Canada
Avec la participation du gouvernement du Canada |  Canadä

*We acknowledge the financial support of the Government of Canada through the
National Translation Program for Book Publishing, an initiative of the* Action Plan for
Official Languages—2018–2023: Investing in Our Future, *for our translation activities.*

Printed and bound in Canada

MIX
Paper from
responsible sources
FSC   FSC® C103567
www.fsc.org

For Jean Bernier, with all my gratitude.

With thanks to Sylvie Sainte-Marie.

Thanks to Sushi, a remarkable artist.

C ome walk with us Mabel, walk between Robbie and me, and tell your parrot to shut it, it repeats everything I say, its echo shrieking when already the roar of the sea is deafening, what is it you're carrying, what's so heavy, Petites Cendres asked, you know what's in the bag, Mabel said, I never would've thought it would be so heavy, the others are going to meet us at Pelican Beach at noon, Robbie said, they're still asleep after going out last night, they probably won't even wake up before eleven, Robbie said, your ginger beers are heavy too, I can carry the bag if you want, Petites Cendres said, no, Mabel said, my old age is a burden too and my legs aren't as young as yours, no, Mabel said, Lena says it should have been me, Angel loved my birds so much, it'll be a grand procession, a huge procession Robbie said, at noon, under the beating sun, I told the whole town to come, Reverend Stone, Dr. Dieudonné,

Dr. Lorraine, it's my people I'm carrying, the poor, devastated Blacks, an ancient people, and the wounds they bear, they'd be crawling on their knees, that's why my knees are wrecked, and you, Petites Cendres, it's like you've lost your memory, that's how it is with you, the next generation, you want to forget, that's how it is, yes, Mabel said, caressing the feathers of the parrot on her shoulder with one hand, but I'd forgotten, you forget how heavy it is, Mabel said, if Lena can find the courage she'll meet us at the beach, she'll come if she can and in the meantime she's crying but it is possible to have enough of weeping, all of a sudden the cup of tears runs dry, yes, Mabel said, I know it, I've known that for a long time, my daughter had her fourth baby you know, Mabel said, Reverend Ézéchielle paid for my plane ticket so I could go see them, it's the fourth time she's done that, some leave this world and others come into it, it's God's will, Mabel said, don't give us that talk about faith, Petites Cendres said, we don't want to hear it, or else pray in your head, okay, but even so, Mabel said, I think God got it wrong, rather than striking you down with His sword, He took Angel, shouldn't you have gone first, Petites Cendres, yet here you are on a day like today, up on your high heels, your belly bare under that flimsy girls' top, your hair in your face and on your cheeks, your flesh is pockmarked by wickedness, but Petites Cendres thought Mabel hadn't actually said those words or else the wind had swallowed them, put them on mute, Petites Cendres thought about his feet burning in his sandals and how good it would feel to jump into the ocean, people were walking past, they were creepy, maybe tourists, heading to a party, they'd pinned masks to their straw hats, animal and fish masks, open-jawed sharks with a thousand teeth, their skin brown with sun, they were

creatures from faraway lands, indifferent clowns in the
funeral procession, Petites Cendres thought, in a minute
they would disappear and the long walk to Pelican Beach
would start once more like a gold chain around Angel's
heart, or like the tumour that had come out of nowhere,
attacking his lungs, how did that happen, no one knew, if
it hadn't been for that horrible dust he would have been
saved, Dieudonné said, holding Lena's hands in his and then
Kitty's and then Misha's paws, Misha whining, the most
sentimental of them, until Dieudonné reminded Petites
Cendres that after all Lena was right there, and Brilliant and
Lucia's birds, and Angel himself was one of the white birds
taking flight each morning toward the egret pond, playing
in the water and flitting around and every day like this the
souls of innocent children fly off into the light, the sky and
the heavens are filled with them, these birds, no, they were
no longer lonely, so Dieudonné said to Misha, the dog
stamping and whining in his young master's bedroom, gazing
up at Dieudonné with bewildered black eyes, black eyes
lost in white fur, where is he and when will he come back
from his voyage out to sea, when, please, why are you lying
to me, he hasn't touched his science books for days and
the fruit his mother peeled for him is sitting on the table,
his mother is catatonic, she can't even move, do you think
I can't see, Misha seemed to say to Dieudonné, suddenly
submissive, he laid a paw on the rainy-day mat, why was
that thing in the house when it was so nice out, Lena tossed
the mat down in the kitchen, Misha, stop following me,
here's your rag, I've got bigger things to think about right
now, and it was true, the fate of mere animals is nothing to
men in times of trouble, and Misha remembered coming
through other calamities, he'd survived them, oh, that was

a long time ago, so long ago, and the one who saved him was a young man, Brilliant, though first the rescuers had saved the women and men and children from the flood and the dogs and cats waited a long time, hanging on to the doors and the wind-torn planks drifting on the water, it had been an apocalypse for the animals, it was, and their masters didn't know where they were, calling them in vain, it was a miracle Misha had been pulled from the water and that he was alive today, yes, but what good was that when Angel had left him, what good was it, what if we went to Pelican Beach, Petites Cendres said to Robbie, we'll do it for Angel, Brilliant used to carry him out there on his shoulders, they would eat together on the sand, in silence, watching the sea, was tonight the night Captain Joë tied up his boat by the beach and called out all aboard, friends, hey, Bryan, I've always got champagne, and this time I didn't steal it, can you hear me, Bryan, even though I'm just a no-good pirate sucking on my hash pipe all day, even though, the words unravelled in the thick air, so hot Angel thought he had a bit of a fever, but it was a feverish happiness, not his health, not what he'd so often felt lying in bed, and Petites Cendres thought it may have been a bad sign that he'd buried a baby bird that morning, tucked it deep into a sandy bush by the pond so Misha couldn't see it or sniff out the little body laid between the layers of earth and sand, wholeheartedly the tiny bird had flung itself against the window, blinded by the glass, the transparency a feint in the sun, a warbler, yellow feathers and brown wings, and taking it in his hand Petites Cendres was struck by how small it was, almost as small as a hummingbird, the hummingbird so small it looks like a buzzing insect, it wears its lightness like a dragonfly sipping at a flower, oh, this bird barely larger than a hummingbird with its trembling wings, the bird he'd buried may have sung its sweet song, Petites Cendres thought, in the forests of northern Louisiana, swept across the black bayous, lakes, swamps, and still-wild country to fly here and finally head off to hotter climes in Cuba, where its brilliant call, scintillating notes rising from its narrow throat, that song would never be heard, was that the music Angel wanted to hear, he wanted them to open the window so it could all wash over him, the heat and the call of the song-exalted bird, but then came the thud against the glass because that morning the doctor had forbidden it, they had to close it, Angel wouldn't be able to breathe, the air was too humid, Angel had coughed a lot during the night, and all he had around him was the cold air of the fans because they'd had to shut the window, that wasn't a good sign, Petites Cendres thought, the closed window, usually it was open so Angel could hear the waves, Atlantic Boulevard, it was the time of day when Misha would ask to go out with Angel on the veranda where flowers bloomed and palm stems tangled into a green arch over the chairs and table so that Misha and Angel could play unbothered under the veiled, soothing sun, they never tired of the sun, Mama had thought of everything, Lena, yes, thought Petites Cendres, everything had been peaceful, before the carnage and chaos no one anticipated, and he wasn't sure Angel could hear the birdsong from the other side of the bedroom, the window closed to keep out the humid air, Dieudonné had said we need lots of blankets to warm him, that's what we need, yes, Angel had said he wasn't cold, open the doors and the windows because his father was coming, more than the song of the yellow warbler it was his father he was hoping to see, Mama had received a letter months before saying what, what had his father said, wouldn't he have come today if he'd been told this day was the last, the most sublime, the sunniest, the day the stars aligned, when the astronauts who'd barely turned twenty were leaving for Mars in their spaceship, they'd been warned it would be a year before they were back if they were lucky enough to come back at all, some of them had signed a contract for life, they didn't want to come home, it was easier for Angel to shut his eyes and imagine Papa wouldn't come today, Papa was a businessman, he travelled a lot, he never had time to stop, that was what his Mama told him, and anyway Angel would be better by nightfall, the doctor had said so, he was tired of fighting his cough and Angel fell asleep, yes that was it, Petites Cendres thought, he'd been able to sleep a while, now Mabel asked Robbie if they could stop on a bench, rest for a few minutes in front of the ocean, she was out of breath, my old legs, you see, and this bag is so heavy, who would've thought it would be so heavy, after the ceremony a boat will be waiting at the pier at noon Robbie told Mabel, and he handed Mabel and Petites Cendres a water bottle that the three of them shared sitting on the bench as skateboarders and cyclists sped past and the freaks with their faces hidden behind shark masks, is that a boat I see, that godforsaken little dinghy out there, Mabel said, men and women and children all piled on top of each other, the waves, the waves, is that what I see, Mabel said, what's out there at this hour are sailboats and yachts, Robbie said, the waves are smaller, but that's not what I see, Mabel said, there's a bunch of silhouettes moving, Mabel said, there on the crest of a wave and then another wave falls and it looks like they're going to go under, Mabel said, wave after wave, I can see them Mabel said, they're wearing orange life jackets and their skin is as black as mine,

Mabel said, I believe they're our African brothers, Mabel said, Reverend Ézéchielle told us in church to pray for them, other than fancy sailboats I can't see anything on the horizon Robbie said, I'm telling you I can see the damned of the earth in a rubber dinghy about to bust Mabel said, Petites Cendres told Mabel she went to church too much, her devotion was a joke, even Reverend Ézéchielle herself isn't that pious, she doesn't even have time to pray, she's too active and charitable, there's always someone who's hungry, a hand reaching out to her, she says, why do you come to me, I can't feed every sparrow or bless every person, the problem is you drink too much beer and do too much coke my children there you have it, Reverend Ézéchielle said, that's why you can't feed your children, all that salt you're snorting, the powder that turns your nostrils pink, do you think I don't know who you are, Bahama Street brats, my fallen beloveds, so spoke Reverend Ézéchielle in her sermons, sometimes she would dance and sing while she preached, Petites Cendres said, it looks like a rubber boat deflating, Robbie said, we see them a lot, these little dinghies, we should call for help, Robbie said, we should help, Mabel said, maybe the shrimpers tonight will see them, they're drifting off, they're farther away now, but I thought they were so close when I saw them, they were yelling and waving their arms and now they've drifted away, Robbie said, here, Mabel, you can't even see them anymore, put down your bag, your heavy bag, and try not to think about it Robbie said, and Daniel thought he was listening to the sound of a concentrated silence, the sober silence of writing around him, he thought as he sat at his desk in the morning, the clamour of dawn gone quiet after the chatter of women's voices, near him Mélanie and Mai were getting ready to go out to sea on Samuel's sailboat so that Mai could go take pictures of the sea turtles, they were an endangered species Mai said, we have to photograph everything quickly, she said, because one day they won't be here anymore and that day is drawing nearer, beneath Mai's seemingly nonchalant demeanour Daniel noticed now that even when the girl smiled at her father or teased him as she used to before, there was the shadow of a rift, almost imperceptible, thought Daniel, which might have affected his daughter's trust or her mood, she was once so natural and relaxed, they'd be back by noon, Mai said, they would go out to the fort today, the Invincible Fortress as they called it, today Mélanie would captain their sailboat, the nimble vessel that had been a gift to Samuel when he was twelve, a boat for the family, it was still called *Southern Light*, thought Daniel, who in his monastic room was about to start writing, Daniel thought that the world went to ruin several times before we woke up in the morning, we caught glimpses of it in our dreams and nightmares as we slept, we learned the world had given way over and over in our slumber, we were outraged, we felt blame and discomfort at living in such a universe, dark and cruel, and then we felt nothing, as if the world was no longer any of our concern, there was a cleaving and we had to go about our business with dignity, that's how Daniel would start writing, he'd see the characters he was describing rise to the surface once more in spite of himself, pushing up out of the dramas of enduring violence he couldn't dispel, on a June morning like this one, a young man, seventeen years old, woke up very early and went down to the basement of his parents' house to inspect his arsenal, the Young Man had an idea in his mind, it had been eating away at him for several months, he'd be rid of them, yes, he would go shoot them where they least expected it, the church was breathtaking, the New Hope Methodist Church, filled with children's choirs and those ministers of God, those pastors on their knees, the Young Man had dreamed of it, standing with his rifle, the butt of the gun under the chin of his cherubic face, and his parents, who never came down to the basement, they thought it was just a workshop for their son's tools there, that he liked to build things, the Young Man's parents, neither religious nor extremists of any denomination, never would have understood the Young Man's idea so he didn't discuss it with them, he'd always been a quiet child, Reverend Antoine had also risen very early that June morning, he had kissed his wife as he rose but would regret later on that he hadn't kissed her tenderly enough, he'd told her over breakfast that their Christian faith would never be strong enough to survive the trials, what trials she asked, my faith is unshakeable, said the reverend's wife, she was a pastor herself, this is what I want to say this morning to my congregation, to those who come to my Bible study, she said, a Christian must have an unshakeable faith, we are not of the same church, Reverend Antoine said, that is a pity, I am Episcopal Reformed and you are African Methodist, in my church doubt is allowed, but isn't that doubt a sign of arrogance, Pastor Anna asked her husband, and they debated at length as they did before heading to church, until Pastor Anna ended their discussion a little abruptly, she didn't want to be late for her classes, the reverend would remember that for a long time, how all at once she wasn't there, by his side, the radiance of the being who was his wife, why hadn't he held her back a little longer that morning in June, all that she was, Anna, whose presence bathed everyone in light, how to explain, Reverend

Antoine would search forever for the words, he hadn't hugged her tenderly enough, affectionately or even passionately that morning, the thought would torment him for a long time, and in his parents' basement the Young Man, taciturn and withdrawn, standing there against his rifle, felt calm, a peace he had rarely known, he felt entirely without blame since the idea had come to him, yes, at last he was at peace with himself, his idea would make him a celebrity, he knew it, even if his celebrity was disgraceful, he would be one of those who dared, that summer in Charleston it had been so hot, so humid, a nagging humidity, the Young Man thought, finally he would be delivered of it, soon, it was so hot he couldn't hunt, couldn't go out and gut some game, there was nothing to do, nothing but think, think over his idea, how he would see them fall one by one and among them the most pretentious with their Bible teachings, it was repulsive, all of it, too bad the summer was so hot, the sweat glued to your skin though he was shivering now, it would be so good to spread terror, dread, it would be, yes, the Young Man's epiphany, for yes, his life, his existence, would have been dull otherwise, it would have been nothing, nothing, he thought, no, nothing but dullness and the taste of blood in his mouth like when you go hunting and nothing remains but nostalgia for the blood that you spilled, and there was never enough, the Young Man thought, the Young Man who was calm now, who was in control of his life, because he had an idea to top them all, he would be the prince of white supremacy, a war divided the white and Black races, it would be so easy, just a slight provocation, shouting I am the warrior who will liberate the white race from the Black, listen to me carefully, it's a war, it's an emergency, I'll slay them all in cold blood, from Missouri

to Maryland, they earn too much already, too much compassion, when they demonstrate on behalf of their dead,
it's alarming, this national movement, it's dangerous for us
poor whites, they'll end up crushing us, defeating us, yes,
thought the Young Man, I'll annihilate them one by one, it's
a good cause, I'll have killed them all by noon, the Young
Man thought, and Daniel suddenly felt so weary writing
down his deeds, it was merely a footnote, a June morning
in the town of Charleston, but the series of scenes with the
Young Man overwhelmed him, the Young Man whose birth
had been bad luck for everyone, but do any of us know,
when we have children, who we are bringing into the world,
what would have become of him, Daniel, if he had been
the Young Man's father, shouldn't we spare the father the
blame for the son's grisly destiny, the Young Man was the
result of trifles of fate, of meaningless chance, his parents,
like all parents, would never have chosen to bring an assassin into the world, and aren't we all the children of chance,
crumbs tossed to the birds with one hand, crumbs like seeds
proving how random it is to be born anywhere, or any way,
and so it was that on this June morning the Young Man
born of inchoate chance seventeen years earlier in the town
of Charleston was now getting ready to go out, today he
had dressed in the grey sweater, black jeans and Timberland
boots the police reports would describe later, and his weap-
ons, a few revolvers, one tucked into the belt of his jeans,
the others in his backpack, it would take a total of seventeen
minutes to finish them off, he thought as he prepared, seventeen minutes in the New Hope Methodist Church where
he would pretend to pray, what would those seventeen
minutes be, bang, bang, bang, as they sang their hymns,
reciting their prayers fervently, don't forget the rifle in the

backpack either, you always have to watch out for the police
dogs, but the Young Man would have time to get away, his
car waiting under the trees along the avenue and he could
run fast, a .45 was the weapon of choice in this situation,
the Young Man thought as he got dressed, the best weapon,
it kills quickly, it is an efficient weapon, they would be in
their Sunday best, perfumed, about to head home for lunch,
potatoes and green beans, and as for the pastor, I will shoot
him first, his wife next, both perfumed, dancing, singing,
and I know they will forgive me, they are so weak, footmen
of God, I don't want them to purify me with their forgiveness, I'd rather be hanged because their forgiveness implies
repentance and I shall not repent, what I want is the whole
congregation, yes, bang, bang, bang, and those arrogant
Black girls I see on the street or playing volleyball with the
white kids, Gracyn, Kaylin, I'll take their father from them,
I will make them orphans, and that other one who dares to
look at me, Nadine, I'll kill her mother too, why not, I should
leave before my folks call me, they're always after me, hey,
why don't you ever eat with your parents, what are you
doing down there that's so important, rebuilding computers
that are of no use, the Young Man emerged from his cave,
armed, his hair freshly cut, he turned his face to the sun
that June morning, his face so clear, not yet ravaged by evil,
yes, thought Daniel, that was how it was, the deed would
soon be done, completed, accomplished, but what surprised
him was that the Young Man, Reverend Antoine would later
say, before the seventeen minutes of killing, before the foul
tragedy in Charleston when all was blood and plunder,
corpses littering the ground, ultimately there would be fifteen
victims in the New Hope Methodist Church, men, women,
the children of the Sunday choir, what an utter tragedy, just

as the Young Man had dreamed in his lusty hunting dreams,
what had surprised him, a few seconds before he became
a killer, was that the Young Man, who attacked the pastor
first, Anna, the wife of Reverend Antoine, this woman who
preached so eloquently, wasn't she haughty, she despised
the Young Man didn't she, he could feel her contempt, there
was nothing worse to him than the contempt of a mature
Black woman for a poor white boy so she had to be his
first victim, what had surprised Reverend Antoine was that
the Young Man showed some reticence, yes, a split second
of reluctance before he shot his wife, she had smiled at him
as if to ask him for grace, mercy, or was it her mysterious
radiance, there had been something inexplicable, the Young
Man for a second almost resisting his ugly, deadly mission,
yes, as Reverend Antoine would say later, he wavered, he
had wavered before his wife's smile but the obsession was
too strong and he fired without warning as if in spite of
himself in a kind of fog, the world smeared with blood, the
mothers of the girls in his class fell at his feet, those stuck-
up girls who played volleyball with the white girls' team
when the white girls always lost, and as he had written in
his manifesto of hate, which fanned out all over the internet
that morning an hour before the crime, the Young Man was
avenging the honour of white people, the poor whites of
America, Charleston and everywhere, today he would be
their hero, the historic decree that had emancipated Blacks
had been a mistake, he wrote, it would have taken another
hundred years of slavery on the plantations and lynchings
for Blacks not to dominate whites like they did today, our
misfortune was that they had learned to read and write,
more often than not from white people after they had fled
to the North to open businesses, schools, even universities,

even as the Young Man's grandfather could barely read and write they had already learned, those pathetic slaves hunched over their cotton got rich and overnight they became the founders of schools and universities, yesterday they had been serfs and today their pockets were lined with the money they'd scrounged, they were building whole towns, always talking about their unconditional love for each other, respect for community, they brought their families from Mississippi to Texas and became entrepreneurs, their numbers swelling so much that families could buy a printing press, they knew that by printing books they would taunt us, our misfortune is that they learned to read and write, the Young Man wrote, the white man should not have sold them a printing press but rope to hang themselves with or guns to kill themselves with before we caught up with them wherever their masters were hunting them down, whipping them and beating them and slamming iron collars around their necks, after all they were our chattel, worthless, while white men toiled away on their plantations, so poor, forever neglected by the government, their wives were giving their husbands their earnings, the women acted like that among the free Blacks, that's how they took our money but when they had their first printing press, think about it, they started selling prayer books, slave memoirs, hymns, songs, they printed and sold up to sixty thousand copies a month, it was in Nashville, that first printing press, a disgrace to us, poor white people who could barely read and write, and bankers, they became bankers too, always challenging us, defying us, and this is why you shall know what I have done, my patriotic action today, I must avenge my people's honour, these were the words of his manifesto of hate and he heard them as he was killing, killing, he was in a fog

where nothing made sense anymore, except that he remembered Pastor Anna's smile, it was as if the sun had pierced
through that slimy fog, her smile, you might have thought
she was his mother and yet he'd had the guts to kill her in
the fog as he waded through, shooting, screaming victory
within himself, the hero of that June morning, yes, that was
how it was on that morning in June, thought Daniel, the
world had collapsed when a white supremacist opened fire
in a Black church, that was how it was, thought Daniel,
when the laws aren't enforced, Robbie said to Petites Cendres
and Mabel, the three of them sitting on the bench facing
the sea, that's how disaster happens, people vote against
us, it's an indelible mark of rejection, of scorn, one of those
assholes said we don't want them here, we don't want you
in our train station and restaurant washrooms, we don't
want them anywhere near us, we don't want to be near
them in the urinals and discover that it's not a man peeing
next to us but a woman, or a man dressed like a woman
but with a penis, no, we don't want any of that in our cities,
in our parks, that's why I voted against them, the man said,
that jerk, Robbie turned to Petites Cendres, who said nothing and sat just breathing the air, why don't you say something, Robbie asked Petites Cendres, nudging him with his
elbow, there are some people who support us, Petites
Cendres said, we have friends, people stand up for us, Petites
Cendres said, even lawyers, not everybody refuses us the
blessing of justice, no, Petites Cendres said, and look, even
Victoire has returned to work as an engineer, she lectures
around the country, she's saved hundreds of transgender
teens, doesn't she always say that there is decency among
men, that none of us would be here otherwise, doesn't she
say, Petites Cendres went on, that the only thing required

of us on this earth is love, oh, man, the jasmine flowers at this time of year, Petites Cendres said, if Angel were with us, he'd be breathing it all in too, yes he would Mabel said, poor child, but the saddest thing, Mabel said, was that once he stopped breathing, the poor child, she said, thumping her chest, Misha didn't want to leave him, he came to lie on his young master, Dieudonné and I couldn't pry them apart, Misha's a big dog, and Dr. Dieudonné said, Misha, be reasonable, Misha, listen to me, Misha grunted, and Lena said let's leave them together a few more hours, let's not bother them, they loved each other so much, it's a sad story, Mabel said, complaining about her knees, her legs, we'll be on our way to Pelican Beach, she said, it won't be long, it's just that this bag is heavy, you know, I promised Lena I'd carry it for her, that I'd go with you to Pelican Beach where Misha and Angel used to run when he was healthy, at least that's a lovely memory, the two of them running together, Mabel said, those who voted against us, Robbie continued, they voted to chastise us and for us to continue to be mistreated, banished, hurt, cursed when we use public restrooms, everywhere we go, Robbie said, it's abuse, it's discrimination and we have to stand up and say so, Robbie said, stop sniffing the air and listen to me, Robbie told Petites Cendres, it has to stop, you need to come with me to the march in San Francisco, you and the other girls, Geisha, Cheng, all of them, Robbie said, I'm too tired, Petites Cendres said, another time, I had the flu last month, the flu in the middle of summer, that's not normal, what do you mean you're tired, Robbie shouted, you know it's because of the coke, not the flu, you liar, may I say something, Mabel said, if you had followed the way of the Lord things would be very different, you'd be accepted everywhere, you'd be

tolerated even in restaurant and bus station restrooms, everywhere, I say, because you would have followed in the
footsteps of the Lord and His straight and sinless path,
Mabel said, but, alas, both you and Yinn and your friends,
you did not follow the way of the Lord, you do not believe
in His sovereign benevolence, Mabel said, moralizing, the
Lord forgives His children, it is written, oh be quiet Mabel,
don't you remember, you're basically our ancestor, our matriarch, don't you remember that not long ago there were
signs, Colored Rest Rooms, don't you remember, doesn't
this seem like the same thing, trans restrooms, don't you
think, Mabel, alas, Mabel said, yes, these are sad things, one
side for Blacks and clean toilets for the whites, I know, I
remember, Mabel said, but I say it's better for both of you
boys to follow the way of the Lord, if only out of caution,
listen to a wise old woman who'd like to see you in heaven
one day, Mabel said, let's get going, Robbie said, and you,
Petites Cendres, shake off your daydreaming, we've got a
long day, and Petites Cendres stood up and noticed the
strange men they'd seen in the morning crowd, wearing
shark masks under their straw hats, they were still there,
walking next to them, who knows if those hoodlums hadn't
been listening in, it worried Petites Cendres, as if they might
have been the ones who'd voted against the bill stipulating
that transgender folks have to be treated with respect, that
they have the right to housing and jobs, that society must
finally end the crimes against them, that they should no
longer be considered second-class citizens in their own
country, yeah, there they were among the cyclists and skateboarders, hidden under their masks, behind the shark teeth,
and Petites Cendres felt exposed, as if they were spying on
him, while by his side Robbie yammered on, Petites Cendres,

you didn't tell me about that flu last month, hey, why didn't you tell me, am I not your brother, your Puerto Rican brother, huh, tell me, oh, no, a pesky cold, a scratch in my lungs, Petites Cendres said, why would I tell you, and besides, you were in Sacramento for a demonstration with Yinn, you're always gone, Petites Cendres said, you march everywhere, both of you, Petites Cendres hesitated, how could he tell Robbie that he'd hardly recognized him and his rhetoric for several months now, Robbie was a hardcore activist, another one drawn in by Yinn, the revolution always running at full boil, quietly though, Buddhist is what Yinn called it, but Robbie in his new role was as flashy as if he were onstage at the Saloon, as if he were some renowned tragic actor, wasn't he pulling away from Petites Cendres, he who could neither travel nor protest, he was always alone, between his hammock in the Acacia Gardens and his sublime birds flying around him as he considered the sky, in that afternoon sky the colour of the emerald sea, as if they had formed an arch above the trees in bloom, Petites Cendres stretching out and into his laziness, into the thought that solitude, so pleasantly populated with his flying angels, his doves, his turtledoves, was what finally appeased his love for Yinn, he loved him too much, and at last he could relax, he could rest, there was plenty of chaos and fear, he thought of the meagre germs threatening to contaminate his body as if he were at the mercy of the slightest venomous breath, yes, in his hammock he could sleep at last, he thought, but Robbie was getting riled up as they walked, listen, so you don't trust me anymore, Robbie was asking him, is that why you didn't tell me, is that it, why don't you come with us, with Yinn and me, as soon as we have a few days off we'll go march and that's why we're alive, you get it don't you, no,

Petites Cendres said, I don't, the true manifestation of courage is when you and Yinn take to the stage, isn't that enough,
as soon as you're onstage at the Saloon you start getting
threats, letters, you put your life in danger, some people
admire you and some people hate you, that's always how
it is, Petites Cendres said, and Robbie said that's why we're
protesting, always how it is, the parrot on Mabel's shoulder
repeated, where are we going, Mama, don't ask so many
questions, Mabel told her parrot, we're going to the sea, to
the pier, to sell ginger beer, Jerry the parrot cawed, yes, like
every day on the pier, Mabel said, be a good boy, Mabel
said, except this time I'm carrying a bag that's really heavy
and Jerry, I'm not telling you what's inside, it would make
you cry, so I'm not telling you anything, while they were
walking along Atlantic Boulevard, the three of them, Petites
Cendres saw a young Black acrobat in tall red boots dancing, wiggling his hips for an audience that didn't seem to
see him, Petites Cendres studied the dancer's thrown-together
look, the mannered sway of his hips, the bounce of his butt
in those indecent shorts, I'm dancing for the sun, the acrobat
said, that's why I swallow fire every day, leaping from one
iron circle to another and I never catch on fire, yeah, I dance
for the sun, I'm a fire-eater, a few bucks in my hat, thank
you ladies and gentlemen, and as the acrobat passed them
Petites Cendres saw the man's mouth was just a reddish
hole, the acrobat was handsome but had no teeth, damn
heroin, Petites Cendres thought again, it destroys them, and
Petites Cendres remembered that he couldn't live without
his dust, so, Robbie said, you want it to speed you to the
grave faster than some infection from that unnameable virus,
you want to look like that guy one day, and while the acrobat was dancing, long legs, his feet clad in those red platform

boots, Petites Cendres thought, yes, what Robbie said was true, he could have tumbled into interminable addictions until he lost his hair, his teeth, but no, I never touch heroin, Petites Cendres insisted, you're too poor, that's why, Robbie said, but your pimps, your customers, those who buy you, cheap, and not even for a whole night because they're in such a hurry to catch their plane, to get away, didn't Yinn tell you there was no need for you to sell yourself, he would have taken care of you at the Acacia Gardens, he could have made an honest man out of you too, a virtuous man, if we can speak of virtue in your case, yes, believe me, your clients could put you up to sinister things, experiment with you, I can defend myself, Petites Cendres said, believe me Robbie, I don't belong to anyone, you're not well, Robbie said, you should stop working, Yinn told me you should be resting, that's all you should be doing, but Petites Cendres was observing Mabel as she walked stoically ahead of him, holding the bag that dragged at her feet, the worst of it, it's not about me, Petites Cendres said, Angel, Angel, Petites Cendres repeated, the worst is that I won't even be able to come visit him in the afternoon anymore, a bit before four o'clock like I used to do every day, that was my routine, visiting Angel with the birds, the worst will be having nothing to do, Petites Cendres said, without Angel, Robbie repeated, yes, that'll be the worst, Petites Cendres said, *Southern Light*, *Southern Light*, Daniel was thinking of Mai and Mélanie sailing on Samuel's boat, the vessel gliding softly along to the rhythm of the waves, there had been a time a few years ago when Daniel used to keep his children close to him on the boat, even Augustino, who, at that time wasn't yet thinking of running away because he loved the water and the light, it was as if Daniel would always see him like that,

swimming with the dogs in the ocean, laughing and mischievous, cockily extending an arm toward his father as he
swam, shouting to Daniel, tell me, Papa, can you swim as
well as I can, hey Papa, you can't swim can you, you're all
about your books, you come out of your cave for an hour
a day to play with your children, tell me, Papa, what do you
think about when you're writing, and Daniel answered from
afar, Augustino, you know I always think only of you, of
you, of my family, you know that, Augustino, do I really
need to tell you every day, I can't be any different, and
Augustino would answer, oh no, Papa, you don't think of
us when you're writing, no, Papa, you forget about us, I'm
sure, your family is elsewhere, and Daniel figured Augustino
was too familiar with his writerly habits, the freedom to
write flashed like a diamond and he was allowed to tear
away from his moorings, even family, Augustino, so young,
was competition, he knew he would soon be a writer himself, very soon, independent of the father he loved, whom
he may even have adored, despite his emotional reticence
with his parents as he grew up, as he became this new,
competitive creature that even his mother Mélanie sometimes
didn't quite recognize anymore, but that's how it was,
thought Daniel, it was the passion of youth that came across,
you didn't always understand your children and Daniel was
self-absorbed as a father, the consequence of his obsession
with writing books and, in truth, he often thought only
about that, even when he was relaxing with his family on
the boat, the *Southern Light*, light of the south, how sweet
the words, and his thoughts drifted with the water moving
with the current and the wind, how glad he was that he
had all his children with him, that not one of them was
absent, even though they used to bicker, Daniel resisting at

that time Mère's suggestion that they send the children to
private school, no, Daniel had decided, Samuel would not
be separated from Venus, with whom he sang hymns at the
Baptist church, Venus, the daughter of Pastor Jérémie, and
it was Samuel, wasn't it, it was comforting to see them
together, they were totally different, wasn't it Samuel who'd
said to his father, Papa, they don't have a boat, they don't
have a big house and a gazebo or a swimming pool like
we do, why, Papa, why don't they have housekeepers like
Jenny and Marie-Sylvie de la Toussaint, how can you explain
these mysteries, Papa, and Daniel hadn't known how to
answer Samuel's questions, saying only that Jenny and Marie-
Sylvie de la Toussaint had been welcomed into their house,
the two young women were refugees, were they refugees
from the sea, Samuel asked, Jenny was studying to become
a doctor, she wanted to join Doctors without Borders, the
position of governess that Mère had conferred on her was
temporary, Daniel told his son, but he knew that the mystery
of rich and poor simply should not be, that it was the most
flagrant injustice, at Venus's house, where the pastor's daughter lived with her brothers and sisters, there were no toys,
Samuel had noticed, lots of children and no toys, because
Pastor Jérémie said praying comes before playing, and even
though there were many children and Venus was the oldest,
her father insisted she was too clever for her own good and
would end badly, the mother kissed the children, even the
thieving boys, said the pastor, she would kiss them and take
them in her arms, as she did with us, only they didn't have
lots of stuff like we did, only an ancient refrigerator sitting
outside in the yellow grass and a bicycle that one of Venus's
brothers had stolen and a scruffy dog named Polly, Daniel
reflected on the things Samuel used to say, the little boy

he'd been when he sang with Venus in the Baptist church, or when they came home from school arm in arm as children do, playing so sweetly, Venus with a hand on Samuel's shoulder, he was only twelve and she was fourteen and she treated him like one of her younger brothers, teasing him, tugging his hair, Daniel could still see their faces, Samuel, Augustino, and Vincent, turning to him aboard the *Southern Light*, Mai wasn't born yet, and he could hear the sound of the waves battering the hull, the boat of which he was master, an awkward captain, someday soon Samuel would take charge, skilfully, his sons so at ease in the world where Daniel only felt his clumsiness, his incompetence, Augustino reproaching him, Papa, you're useless, writing's all you're good at, let me help you, Papa and, in his cumbersome fatherhood his sons did help him, yes, it's true, he thought, he was always preoccupied with what he would write that day, that night, the next, except when it came to Vincent, he'd taken him to the hospital so many times, his condition kept getting worse, to the point that he would almost suffocate, lose consciousness, he'd have to quickly tie up the boat at the marina, Mélanie had cried so much when Vincent was born because she knew, right away she knew this child was destined to suffer, the contractions, the pain, for days she'd secluded herself with Vincent as if she were in mourning, Daniel remembered the blinds lowered against the bright daylight and, in the room, Jenny and Marie-Sylvie at the door, her Vincent panting, struggling to breathe, her Vincent who would never be like the others, her child blighted and stricken, but unexpectedly morning came and dried Vincent's tears, dawn rose on the child's joy and the mother's gratitude, she felt him reborn, yet another time Vincent had survived, and Jenny and Marie-Sylvie came into

the room and hurriedly opened the blinds to let in the sunny
day, you see, Mélanie, Jenny said, he's better now, let's head
out by the water while the sun isn't too strong, but Mélanie
was drained, she'd been so afraid for the child and she
stayed in bed, it's over, repeated Jenny, come with us,
Mélanie, Mélanie, come with us, how many nights, how
many days and nights had been wasted in the shadow of a
disease that seemed incurable, no one able to offer any
specifics or reassuring words, how often had Daniel held
his son, forever his boy, against his heart, wondering for
how long they would get to keep him, will he be with us
tomorrow, that boy was a man now, and healthy, he had
overcome everything, Vincent was the most reserved and
guarded of their children, and the one who would captain
Samuel's boat, take the helm of the *Southern Light*, sail only
when the sea was calm and a southeasterly wind filled the
sails, avoiding the north winds and stormy days when the
boat might run aground in the mangroves where pelicans
winged slowly and iguanas swam beneath the grasses showing only their green heads, but his life would be difficult,
nothing easy or complacent about it, Vincent, Vincent had
been saved but his whole life would be devoted to his young
patients, to his research on pediatric respiratory diseases
and from one day to the next Daniel stopped seeing much
of him, though he hadn't just disappeared as, inevitably,
Augustino had done, or should they instead consider it
miraculous to have known Augustino at all, whether he'd
left for good or not, whether or not he had deserted the
comfort of his birth, of his life, was it miraculous to know
that he was writing books even as his parents despaired in
his absence, it was amazing, really, that he'd managed to
evade them, that he'd escaped from everyone, their prodigal

son so rebellious as to be unapproachable, he who most assiduously condemned the privileged class to which he and his family belonged, and his grandmother too, the grandmother he'd loved so much, *Southern Light*, thought Daniel, leaning over the words as he wrote, it was only later that evening in June when the Young Man's parents recognized their son on television, the camera showed the interior of the church of those who would perish that morning, that same indifferent camera revealed the identity of the murderer to the Young Man's parents, it was him on the television, their son, yes, they said, he'd been wearing a grey sweater that day, and dark jeans, that was him, their son, those boots, they recognized the Young Man's boots, what had he done this time, where was he, yes, it was him, a .45, yet how was this even possible, the Young Man's parents had no guns at home, it was a .45, that the first detail that surprised them, baffled them, the FBI will be here soon to question us, our son, is it really him, tomorrow he'll appear before a judge in a prison uniform, no, no, that's not our son, we don't know anything about the Young Man, the boots, yes, but the grey sweater, the delicately feathered shock of hair across his forehead, that's not our son, but look, a pair of armed officers standing on either side of him, right and left, our child, no, he is no longer ours, thought the Young Man's parents, a judge, a white man on their side would defend them, oh, the Young Man's parents are no different from you, pastors and wives of pastors, they too are victims deserving to be pitied, today they have lost their son, he's doomed, he'll be executed, just as you have lost your husbands and daughters, have pity on parents who have suffered such an affront to their dignity, have pity on this family, and the children of the victims, and the sons and the wives of the pastors and the husbands of the women killed in the massacre, but they cried out no, we cannot take pity on his parents, it is our blood that was shed, the blood of our fathers, of our mothers, of our daughters, God in His goodness can bestow His holy mercy upon them but as for us, no, enough, we feel only horror for your son and in any case, you know as well as we do that your white son will not be executed, if he'd been Black then he would not have been spared, you know that, fifteen charges of hate crimes should carry the death penalty for your son but no matter how atrocious his acts were he will not have to suffer that fate, we'll strive for forgiveness because our religion tells us to forgive, we are against capital punishment because to be in favour of it is to be as criminal as the young man who killed our people and we do not want to be as bad as he is, God gives life and takes it, it is up to God to judge him, it will be up to God, not us, and in his cell the Young Man heard this message but felt no remorse and the expression on his childish face vacillated between fear and revenge, he slept in a dirty, smelly bed that June night and someone said you could hear him weeping until an unfamiliar slumber came over him, as if he had fallen, stunned, into a void, the crying persisted every night of his imprisonment and for a long time he sobbed, like a whiner, a weakling, a narcissist, wailing over his fate on cold nights bereft of conviction or redemption because according to Daniel God had no mercy for such crimes, unless the tears were genuine, which was doubtful, though maybe the Young Man felt the smile of Pastor Anna graze him that first night in June, her smile before he fired a few rounds at her, holding her hostage at the end of his rifle, had he heard her say Young Man, you don't have to do this, you don't, go back to your parents, it's not too late, go back, please go back, and didn't he scream your men rape our women, you invaded our country, my country, I have no choice, I must do what I must do, and at the same time he'd heard the voice of a girl, Mama, Mama, I think I'm going to die Mama, Mama, I'm bleeding, I think he hit me Mama, and at last, after ninety seconds, there was silence, he remembered it so clearly, how irritated he'd been by the bodies littering the ground, the Young Man walked among them, crushing a foot with his boot, or a dying hand, he'd screamed once more, stop crying, shut up, shut up, do you want me to start shooting again huh, is that what you want, bang bang, I have more bullets, bang bang bang, Pastor Anna's inscrutable smile hadn't deterred him in the slightest although on that June night, his first night in maximum security, the Young Man thought back on the woman who'd resisted until she fell, and until he himself felt shivers of horror, for at last he had done what he must, so it was, it was inevitable, it could not have been otherwise, and as Daniel wrote, he could see figures from his own past coming at him, Samuel as a child with Venus always at his side, at church and at school, they sang together everywhere, in the choir or as a duet, their voices were so inspiring, the blond boy and the Black girl, and when a schoolboy's wicked hand launched a stone at Venus and her dress was torn, her white Sunday dress, she shouted at her tormentor you'll be well punished for this, one day white men will kneel before me and they will be at my beck and call, you'll see, you'll see, soon I'll be singing at my uncle's club, my uncle is a Korean War vet, and white men will go mad with desire, you vile seed, I spit on you, go home to your mother, I curse the woman who gave birth to you, Venus's anger poured forth like a raging sea, and it washes

over us still, thought Daniel, the earth, the universe bore
her anger, there would be no respite, no calming shore for
the wrath of Venus, thought Daniel, I live in a shack, a
shabby green shack crushed beneath a pale sun, she told
Samuel, I have to get out of there, my father's voice is weighing me down, Pastor Jérémie, man of God, always right, we
will always be poor and my brothers are thieves, I want to
be rich, I want to live, to get away from that shack and own
a real house one day, get away from the rough, chicken-
pecked patch of lawn, I want to be respected, and you'll
see, Samuel, they will kneel before me because I will be
beautiful and powerful, you will see, Samuel, on Sundays
Venus sang and danced in the temple while her father
declared in his sermon that the trumpets of the Lord would
make the earth tremble, and Venus danced and sang on the
rough grass while roosters and hens cackled in the garden,
you don't know a thing, Robbie said to Petites Cendres as
they walked along by the sea, you, a half-blood dressed in
women's clothing, what do you want your future to be, they
don't want people like you anywhere, though you're not
completely the wrong colour you'll never have a steady job,
you'll never have medical insurance, you live totally in limbo,
how many more times will you be assaulted, insulted, tell
me, you incite violence and murder, that's the truth of it,
Robbie said, and that doesn't shock you, your parents don't
greet you when they pass you on the street, you lie daydreaming in your hammock with your birds and you refuse
to come with us to protest in San Francisco, and Petites
Cendres replied that although he didn't work much, he did
have a steady job, the steadiest job in the world, but yes,
his clients were sadistic and stingy, too bad, he said, I can
see them on the boat, Mabel said, they'll fall overboard,

Mabel said, I bet they can't even swim, Mabel said, there are women and small children, Mabel said, may God in His goodness watch over the wretched, over them Mabel said, she was running out of breath keeping up with Petites Cendres and Robbie, if you were honest folks like me, Mabel said, then you wouldn't have so much to worry about, I pray every day and when I get to heaven I will pray for both of you, Mabel said, oh shut up, enough of your pieties, Robbie said, I'm talking about change, about revolution, about total social upheaval, about teaching the masses compassion and Mabel you're rambling, no I'm serious, Mabel said, think of me as your mother, or even your grandmother, do you think Lena will come join us at Pelican Beach, there'll be singing and lots of music, Eureka will be there with the Black Ancestral Choir, poor Eureka who won't be soaping up her baby's hair anymore, she cried a lot, Eureka did, but Christian that she was she said he was already an angel playing the harp at the feet of our Lord for Jesus loves little children, of course, Robbie sneered, he loves them so much he eats them right up, it's make-believe, Robbie said to Mabel, Angel's father wrote to Lena that he didn't want hymns or prayers, he's an atheist, they're not the same religion, Lena is Catholic and wants a lot of singing, lots of songs for Angel, that's how it is, Mabel said, when the parents aren't the same religion then they are enemies, Mabel said, what's the use of marrying if you're going to fight, cast a shadow over your child's entire life, Petites Cendres said, it made Angel so unhappy, Petites Cendres said, to think I won't be able to see him every day right before four o'clock, my days won't be as full any they were, full, full of what, what were your days full of, Robbie asked, air and sun and lazing in a hammock, that's what your days are full of,

Robbie said to Petites Cendres, and you're not even principled enough to march with us, me and Yinn, you'd take abuse over dignity, really, I've never come across that before, Robbie said, and on top of it you never mentioned anything to me about the flu last month, as if I wasn't your friend, your Puerto Rican brother, come on boys, don't fight so much, Mabel said, Jerry's getting angry, the parrot was hopping from one leg to the other, I adopted them together, Mabel sighed, Merlin and Jerry, they were inseparable, nuzzling up against each other with their beaks, animals are capable of love you know, friendship, more than we are, oh yes, Mabel said, more than we are, more than we are, Jerry repeated, rubbing himself against Mabel's neck, she was looking at the sky, clear blue, thinking she needed to walk slower in the beating sun because otherwise her feet would swell, and the bag was getting heavier and heavier, it's true that despite being bedridden Angel had grown a lot in recent months, when she came to bathe him Eureka would call him her long-legged baby as she wrapped him up in the blue towel, she came more and more frequently because of the fever, Angel's high fevers, let's sing a hymn, some gospel to put you to sleep, and she sang, that's how you chase away the fever, with singing, yes, close your eyes now, and during the June nights' harrowed sleep the Young Man gradually became used to the cramped confines of his cell, and to the nightmares, the Young Man reflecting on his big idea, his idea, full of optimism, the glorification of the white race, he would escape from prison, the politics and parties of white nationalism were obsolete, what they needed was a new party of hate, he'd start one as soon as he was released, a wicked spark had revived him, he would be the party's founder, the White Supremacist Youth, he would summon young people to join him, thousands of young people were unemployed, he'd be able to talk to them and invite them to join the party, he would convince them, can't you see who's oppressing you, he would say, can't you see that you are superior to them in rank, in the colour of your skin, we'll burn down their shacks as we did in the past, bomb them out, tar and feather them, there'll be lynchings, we'll hang them from the trees, we the White Supremacist Youth shall preserve the purity of our traditions, do we even have a choice given that they want to dominate us, no, we by our sovereign will shall destroy them, and not just fifteen in a church, no, from now on we shall slay them by the hundreds, by the thousands, we shall disappear them and won't have to listen to their soul music or their Jamaican reggae, no longer shall we be an underground movement, we'll be seen and heard, yes, and mark them with these three letters, WSY, White Supremacist Youth, we'll silence their voices, their hymns, their songs, their prayers, finally we shall reclaim our country and our rights, and I shall be the movement's founder, yes, the White Supremacist Youth, and muttering these words at last the Young Man fell asleep and, that same June night, as he ensconced himself into the abomination of his callous slumber, young girls, twelve-year-old girls running from the ruthless creed of their rapists fled toward a refugee camp in the mountains of Kurdistan, they should be there by morning, there were others who hadn't been able to follow, others who were too small, the men's prisoners, men who prayed before raping them, little one, it's no crime to rape you, my faith commands it, let me bind your hands, it is my right, don't you see how devout I am, I pray before and afterwards, here I am on my knees by your bed and still praying, raping you brings me closer to God, it is God's will, and the girls who'd managed to flee bolted like gazelles toward the crest of the purple hills, they had escaped, what an affliction it was for the children of a religion other than his own, they were the Yazidi minority and they would be raped and killed, that young man who was also seventeen years old had many brothers, yes, our theology is radical and ferocious but that is as our God decrees it, and all must bend to our ways, to our teachings, no matter how young, heretics and infidels and unbelievers will be our captives, this is how we will build our empire, our followers will recruit and sell the girls to our soldiers, and that fifteen-year-old raped by one of the fanatical militants on Sinjar Mountain was sold to an Iraqi fighter, see her mortification, see how we defiled her, we believe they must be punished and defiled, that is the way, see us everywhere standing with our flags, on top of Sinjar Mountain and elsewhere, and Daniel thought of the rape of these children, the world collapsing each night while we slept, and he held on to the image of a fleeing girl, a girl in red, sandals on her feet, a twelve-year-old girl so determined that she found protection in a refugee camp in the hills of Kurdistan and who, turning her face away from us, stared at the barbed wire and, beyond the gates of the camp, the mountains purple in the breaking light, it was as if Mai had been near him in the wounded body of that young girl, Mai at twelve, her life completely different than this one and as he thought of Mai he was sure he could hear gentle waves, the sea was calm today, rocking Samuel's boat, the *Southern Light* upon the ocean, carrying it toward Mélanie and Mai sailing hand in hand among the islands, Woman Island and Man Island, which separated them from Old Uncle Isaac's island, the Island

No One Owns, so called by Isaac because he wanted his
island to be welcoming for everyone, especially poets and
artists, an island that belonged to no one, there was a string
of peaceful islets and a sort of marine park for sea turtles
and birds and endangered fish, that was where they planned
to sail that morning if the winds stayed calm, and the hum
of the waves soothed Daniel's throbbing heart, Daniel who
would have preferred to forget what he had just written,
the slow massacres he'd described, writing day and night,
Mélanie and her daughter Mai believed in the salvation of
humanity though Daniel had his doubts though he was
neither jaded nor disillusioned, how could he be so guarded
that he couldn't join them in their amazement before the
beauty of the world, their delighted contemplation of sea
turtles, eaglets, the majestic birds soaring over the mangroves, as if this had been the beginning of the world rather
than its approaching end wrought by our own appetite for
destruction, and the *Southern Light* was gliding through the
water in a covey of white pigeons and egrets, majestic, the
boat drifted toward sandy beaches where the sea turtles
that spent most of their time in the water came to sleep on
the rocks in the sun, and dolphins and young sharks circled
the *Southern Light* and in this seascape of water and light
nothing seemed to be able to upset Mélanie and Mai's happiness, look, Mai said to her mother, look at the dolphins,
Mother, see how affectionate and confident they are, above
all we mustn't scare the young sharks, no, the balance of
nature is so perfect here, later Mai would tell her father how
they had released a turtle stuck on a rock and caught up in
plastic ties, how there were pieces of glass in the yellow
and red ears of the striking animal, sea turtles can live to
fifty years, Mai said, but their lives are cut short by plastic

waste pinning them to a rock, condemning them to an agonizing death but this time Mélanie and Mai had released the sea turtle back into the water and Mai had felt an intimacy with this endangered animal that linked her to the dominion of animal life, how is it that we accept life can be consumed like this, broken, like this sea turtle which might have been deprived of a future, Mai and Mélanie, thought Daniel, because they were women, felt even more than he did an urgency that the chain of life shouldn't be constantly wounded and rent, they knew this instinctively because without women there would be no future, although Mai was in the habit of telling her mother that in a world of so much more violence than love she didn't want to have children, but Mai's thoughts were never set, she changed from day to day, her evolution sometimes accelerated and sometimes slowed down by what she witnessed around her, every day her observation of the universe ranged from piercing to tender before the spectacle of our time, when so many adult souls lost their way, Mai kept a closed door on her secrets, she never spoke, for instance, of Manuel, who was back from Lebanon, nor about the arrest of his drug-trafficker father, the adventure had marked her but Mai said nothing of the forbidden world she had discovered with Manuel and his father providing teenagers with drugs at parties at his oceanfront estate, what do we ever know about the sexual conflicts of our children, thought Daniel, we only see it bloom on their faces and then, as with Mai, the door slams shut, because the spontaneity of youth is so naturally sunny that, as with Mai, it can look like fulfillment, which is little more than a fragile semblance of happiness, what made Mai appear fulfilled was her vigour, her energy, boisterous and infectious to those who lived near her,

compared to this child so energized by life Daniel was more
sombre, brooding over the Young Man and the murder of
innocents in the church, he remembered that the Young
Man did not walk on his sinister journey alone, violent youth
were lighting fires everywhere, infernos like the flames of
the Inquisition, and the triumph of collective cruelty, the
voices of incendiary youth and of the apparatus of destruction encroaching upon countries and cities would gradually
bury any spiritual or artistic growth in an unholy tumult in
which nothing human could survive for long and art would
die, and a voice instructed the Young Man to get up, rubber-
gloved hands slipping a bowl between the bars, time to eat,
the voice said, and the Young Man saw the hands reach
between the bars of his cell and he knew it was true, he
was no more than a common criminal, a prisoner, where
had the hero of that June morning gone, where was he
when in prison there were only the shouts of men, so much
screaming, and the stench, he wanted to pry apart the bars
and run away, yes, and what a horrid uniform he had to
wear in his cell, people were so afraid to touch him they
came to serve him his lunch with gloves on, he was untouchable, he too had that smell now, the smell of murder, the
smell of blood, the smell of his crimes, it was his now too,
as if after a hunt he had been hosed down in his jeans,
sweater, and boots, the Young Man looked around disdainfully, what was there to see in the gloom, a crude steel
object that was the toilet bowl and a urine-splattered sink,
he was only allowed a visit from his parents once a month,
he didn't want to see them, their sad eyes, all that time in
the basement, what were you doing, tinkering you said, and
we never noticed that you'd accumulated a whole arsenal
though it's true, we never went down below, we let you rot

there with your fixation on revolvers, on guns, it's true we turned a blind eye so what happened is our fault too, we pretended you didn't exist, you were a stranger to us, and the Young Man believed he heard his parents say these words, he was cold and hungry but refused to go near his bowl and its reek of rotten soup, but he knew that his parents, struck dumb with horror, wouldn't say a word, and as the judge who'd come to their defence said, including them among the victims, the crooked white judge who'd avoided denouncing the murderer because he was white, the Young Man's parents were in spite of everything to be pitied, they could be counted among the victims, the staggering number of victims, and the Young Man knew he would appear before another judge who would be intransigent, no doubt a Black man who would demand the death penalty and nothing less, unless that judge was very religious, the Young Man thought, the hatred gripped him, but he was barred from contact with the other inmates and he had all the time and solitude in the world to consider his project, his big idea of one day seeing the end of the Black and yellow races, of brown people, he hated them so much, he had time, oh yes, he thought, so full of hatred he shook with it, but he was also hungry and the smell of his meal wafted toward him even as he was wracked by hatred and anger, and Daniel contemplated how, when he was writing, day or night, he was seized by a persistent dream that seemed to dissipate in Augustino's absence, it was some time ago, after the international literary festival of writers for peace in Scotland, he'd returned home after a long flight looking forward to seeing his family but no one was in the house, every room was empty, not Mère nor Mélanie nor the children, no one was waiting for him and a cold silence stretched

out before him, he called them one by one but no one
answered and the hum of the waves rose up in the quiet,
it was during a storm, the windows of the house were open
to the tumult of the sky and Daniel walked with difficulty
to Augustino's room, the door closed, no one was allowed
to go in, and finally Daniel crossed the threshold into the
room, the objects seemed to be carrying on living Augustino's
erstwhile life, his books neatly arranged on the shelves and
his manuscripts piled up on his work table, so he is here,
thought Daniel, his son had been writing just a few minutes
earlier, and Daniel called to him but he didn't answer, Daniel
feeling that Augustino was very near, near enough to hear
him breathing, outside the storm was winding down, and
inside a cold, indifferent silence paralyzed Daniel in this
place that was no longer his house, his family had abandoned it, every room was tidy and the most surprising thing
was that although the house felt so alive Mai's menagerie
was nowhere to be found, her animals on the armchairs
and sofas, the cats, dogs, birds, Daniel was so used to them
and he looked after Mai's pets as much as she did, especially
now that she lived in another city, even the animal presence
offered no comfort, and when he woke up he quickly wrote
down his dream, it would come back to haunt him, and it
seemed as if the dream was not only about Augustino but
also about his own uncomfortable position in the powerful,
violent winds disturbing the universe of his household,
where fate had designated him a place with his family in a
very specific location on earth, his island, where he feared
a deadly shipwreck would come to pass, his people lost,
like the daily shipwrecks that were graves for countless
others in the Middle East and elsewhere, graves for a multitude of young lives, and Daniel woke up thinking how

surprised he'd been, despite his constant searching for Augustino, to see the son he never expected coming up to him at that festival in Scotland, the son they'd neither expected nor hoped for opening his arms to his father as Daniel came off the stage, notes still in hand, dissatisfied, berating himself for an awkward presentation, it had been too dense, and among the rest of the applauding writers, they shared his passion for a peaceful world, yes, could it be real, there was Vincent, coming toward him and saying, Papa, I wanted to surprise you, that poem of Mai's you read at the end is moving and true, don't kill us, young people don't want to die in your nuclear gloaming, she's so right, what she wrote is so right, I'm so glad you quoted her, Papa, and for everything you said, I listened to you so closely, I have several doctor colleagues with me too, we wanted to be here too because many of us care for the victims of war beyond our own borders, and Daniel was about to cry as he listened to his son, how eloquent he is, though he speaks so little, he's usually so reticent, and what a kindness, to come all the way here to this Scottish forest when he has such a busy schedule at the hospital, to travel so far away, so much palaver for a father he normally saw so seldom because of his profession, Vincent, my unknown son, thought Daniel, standing here before my eyes when Augustino may never return, who knows, although I never stop waiting, I think only of him, and he recalled too the boy Vincent had been, through untold crises, Vincent, whom he'd managed to save just barely so many times, Vincent, who was now a man, and he noticed his son's short hair, how conservative he looked beneath his restrained enthusiasm, their only son with short hair, such a serious countenance amid the throng of writers rambling in the forest after the event, in his black

jeans and white jacket Vincent seemed to belong to the
group of writers, Daniel wouldn't even have noticed him
had he not lifted a hand saying, Papa, it's me, Vincent, do
you have any news, Papa, the writers from Iran, Africa, the
ones that you were waiting for tonight, where are they, Papa,
and they talked for a long time and Daniel thought that if
he had lost Augustino he had found another child here and
this one loved and admired his father profoundly, he had
no idea how guilty Daniel had felt for so long for not having
been able to help his sick child enough during the first years
of his life, he'd done his best, he thought, he'd found excellent doctors for his son though for some time they'd said
that Vincent, with his bouts of choking, his spells that verged
on the comatose, that Vincent would never recover, yet as
soon as his condition improved it was impossible for his
father to keep him from playing, he was reckless, he leapt
into life, an intrepid reclaiming of the days that was almost
too much, Mélanie didn't want him to play sports but it was
no use, that was all he wanted to do, swimming and water-
skiing as soon as he had learned to control his attacks,
which he did with such willpower and courage, and yet the
respiratory problems Vincent suffered from the moment he
was born had scarred Daniel, who tried to atone for the
pain with compassion, the pain of innocents, Vincent among
them, and while he was so grateful to see his son, popping
up before him at the big literary festival in Scotland, writers
for peace at the top of a mountain in the middle of the night
in the fall, because the event had been held into the evening
and through the night, it had been interminable actually,
the invited writers raising a multitude of issues in their
muddled dreams of a better world, the discussions had no
end, they couldn't wrap it up with some conclusion to fix

or mitigate the issue, no, these dramatic questions about the future would remain unanswered, how could there be answers or closure when in some countries writers agitating for liberty were punished with a hundred lashes, the writers' discussions were suspended in a perpetual state of alert because the freedom to write was only granted to some and others paid for their words with years of imprisonment, exile, floggings, thought Daniel, and so while he was delighted to see Vincent at his side Daniel couldn't help but think of the times he'd been a coward in the face of his son's frailty, his illness, his breath short and so quickly depleted, as if he were embarrassed at being this way in front of others, was it during that time that he would hardly go anywhere with Vincent, while the boy's mother, on the contrary, took him out everywhere in his tiny wool outfits, took him to see their friends, cherished him more than her other children, Daniel took him out in Samuel's boat but always so cautiously, studying the winds and the tides, there was a disgrace in sickness, a persecution that Daniel took personally, a form of cowardice he couldn't forgive himself, and as he looked at Vincent's open face, the joy of seeing him, surprising his father in a room full of writers where of course Daniel had not expected him to appear, and at that moment Daniel thought of James, his parents called him J'aime so that their son would never forget how much his parents loved him, Daniel had watched J'aime grow up with his own children because his parents owned a restaurant with a terrace overlooking the sea and the wide beach, and Daniel brought his family there because they loved the roosters, the chickens, the cats that roamed loose, his children loved animals, and that's how come Daniel often saw J'aime sitting on a blue bench beside his mother, Daniel always with a twinge of guilt, it was hard to look at the body contorted by cerebral palsy and Daniel would try to turn his gaze away from J'aime, but J'aime, who wanted to become a poet, a writer, he was so taken with Daniel, and he would stare at him with his bewitching blue eyes, eyes so expressive that Daniel could only look at the boy and ask J'aime, is it true, James, that you want to be a poet, no, J'aime, my name is J'aime, the young boy replied with his eyes and with his whole body, the flailing of his arms and legs, either a poet or a film critic because Mommy takes me to see the movies, don't you, Mom, and J'aime's mother, who had her son's striking eyes though hers were sadder, she said her son was so smart it frightened her and would Daniel be so kind as to look at his poems, his stories, it may sound crazy but I'm sure my son is a poet, he's learned several languages, we can't leave him alone, there are hoo-ligans all over the place in this city, but Mom, you have to leave me alone, I don't need to be dragged around in my wheelchair anymore, I'm fine on my own in the city, people are polite and respectful, come on Mom, stop trying to protect me, and it's true, thought Daniel, J'aime, like Vincent, was a lesson in courage, because at eighteen J'aime went out, he was independent, wheeling himself with his fumbling fingers to the library, to bookstores in the city, alone at last, he said, without parents behind him or else a guardian, a friend of the family, he would go alone to the movies too, and Daniel came to meet him, with less of his ridiculous embarrassment because J'aime, with his radiant smile, and an analytical intelligence emanating from phrases stilted by the twists of his body, no longer represented pain, it was as if his spirit had the power to unshackle him from the body he was chained to, his subtle, superior mind captive

from birth, J'aime belonged to a human species more luminous than Daniel, if God existed, but He couldn't exist, He
had inflicted on J'aime that dreadful punishment of a body
continually distended by pain, confined to a wheelchair, an
angel smiling at everyone, asking everyone how are you
today, I'm going to the library to write my short stories,
they're autobiographical, J'aime would explain, and then
I'll see a movie at the theatre this afternoon, do you know
anyone freer than me, and reading the stories the young
author had entrusted to him, a book that would later be
published, Daniel had sensed in J'aime's words fears he
never spoke of, one of which was that as he went about in
the streets, to the library, to the movies, J'aime would
encounter hooligans who would knock him down on the
pavement, what would he do, upside down and unable to
get up, at the mercy of their blows, but soon in his stories
his fear was replaced by pleasure, the pleasure of learning
a new language by watching videos at the library because
he wanted to go with his parents to Italy, to Spain, he wanted
to know everything, to understand everything, because
according to J'aime the world was beautiful, and who knows,
thought Daniel, he may well have been right, and as Daniel
listened to his son's voice that night in Scotland, their two
faces, Vincent's and J'aime's, became one, yes, he thought,
boys like them were of a completely different species, pur-
veyors of light when others less noble exist to spread darkness, and as the Young Man listened to the howls, the shouts
pouring from the prison cells, the racket was astounding,
night and day, he was sequestered, he could only leave his
cell accompanied by two armed guards, he inspired the
same terror in everyone and would for several months, he
thought, before his trial, as he walked with the guards,

handcuffed, to his medical assessment, a psychologist would tell everyone that he had lost his mind or that his actions had been caused by early dementia, that he was hallucinating, insane, what might they say to spare him the death sentence, he wondered, the prison psychologist was a Black man, and immediately the Young Man despised this man trained to analyze troubled abysses of violence, he would have liked to take the fruits a gloved hand had brought him with his bowl that morning, an apple, a pear, and toss them, throw them at the Black man's face, the man was pushing him to anger, rage, what was it he'd said to him as he walked between the two guards, the execution chamber is at hand, by death row, at the end of the hall, where men await their ultimate punishment, we don't yet know if you will be spared this punishment, we do not yet know anything, whether you consciously committed these heinous crimes, you're young but you'll be tried as an adult, the psychologist was patient, notebook in hand, as you await your day in court, pray, pray, he repeated to the Young Man but as the guards took him back to his cell the Young Man said to them I don't want to see that man, I spit upon him, I am a white nationalist, though I don't belong to any gang, I know there are supremacist gangs out there but I represent a new movement, I don't want to join the old men festering in here, and the guards locked the door to the cell where he would remain in solitary confinement, they left, ignoring his ramblings, and the Young Man felt the cold of the cell crawl under his orange numbered suit and his skin, he thought about what the psychologist had told him, death row, the execution chamber, it would be better to feign insanity, to claim to have been mentally deranged when he appeared before the judge, that would be better, and he lay

down on the putrid mattress thinking about the men condemned to death who also lie on beds, strapped in before
the lethal injection, before their time, and finally he shut his
eyes thinking none of it could be true, it couldn't be true,
since that morning in June when he had stopped to pray
in a church his life had been a nightmare, and it was the
psychologist who had reminded him that he'd mingled with
the congregation for a few moments to pray with them
before he'd killed them all, men, women, children, and that
pretense of praying before slaughter, hadn't that been the
most sinister ruse, the most appalling, hypocritical act, I
wanted to know if you were even aware of it, the psychologist asked, I was hesitating because of a woman, the Young
Man replied, that woman was Pastor Anna, she had given
you a maternal look, yes, the Young Man said to the psychologist, it was that kind of look, because of that woman
I hesitated and yes, I joined in the farce of their prayers, I
was singing with them and thinking, yes, this morning is
either the most holy or the bloodiest of my life and when
Pastor Anna smiled his way and said it's not too late, go
back to your parents, you must not commit such abomina-
tions, when he was about to shoot her, he hesitated before
he shot her several times, shouting, your husbands rape our
wives, white women, they rape our girls, that's why it's my
duty, I must accomplish my mission, bang, bang, and the
slimy fog rolled in, it was disgusting, those bodies bleeding
together, falling among the votives in the church, and the
last one who smiled at him, Pastor Anna, he didn't quite
know how he had bloodied her chest, where had the bullet
come from, you must remember, the psychologist said, if
you hesitated, it was because you were conscious of the
murders, the revenge fantasy you'd held on to for so long,

because your spirit had been hungry for evil for a very long time, can't you admit it, hungry, yes, which means these criminal acts were premeditated and that makes you guilty, you'll need to defend yourself before the judge, you had premeditated this carnage in your parents' basement for a long time, isn't that right, the psychologist asked, and the Young Man answered I was born like this, detesting the lot of you, the colour of your skin, your fleshy voices, aware that he was insulting the Black psychologist, your smell, I was born hating you because you invaded our land, you were our slaves and now you're everywhere, when I was born I felt I had lost my country and it was your fault, the way you have of imposing yourselves everywhere, your fancy jobs, you've crushed poor whites like my grandfather, they didn't know how to read and they had to go to work on your plantations, you robbed us, stripped us, oh, yes, the Young Man's tone was shrill and the psychologist sent him back to his cell, the two guards in charge of him were colossal and the Young Man feared them, it felt as if these two men would be present at his execution, that they were there to walk him to the end of the hallway they called death row, and where, in the suffocating isolation of the prison, the condemned awaited the day their sentence would be carried out, prisoners would never leave these walls, the dead in waiting, and what's with your hair, your bangs layered like that over your forehead, you look like a child, why such vanity before such an atrocity the psychologist asked, and the Young Man replied that he wanted to look respectable that June morning because he would be on television, in the newspapers, along with his manifesto of hate his face would be posted on the internet, he wanted to look respectable, yes, he said, to carry out my mission, I wanted the moment to be historic, a great day, yes, but the psychologist, whom the Young Man hated for the colour of his skin, was digging, digging into the wound of his past as if he had the right, as if he had the power, the Young Man didn't care, though wouldn't he be better off giving in to the psychologist's pressures if he was there to get him a lighter sentence, so when the psychologist asked when he had witnessed these rapes, could you describe them to me, he said a white jogger was running in a park in my city, she was assaulted and raped by four Black men, now the Young Man was lying, recounting an incident that had happened elsewhere, not in a park in his city but another park in New York, and it had been proven that the four men were innocent of the rape, but the psychologist was on to him, he knew the Young Man was lying, nice try clever guy, he would make him talk, one session at a time, yes, the Young Man would end up confessing when in his childhood and adolescence the racism and hatred had taken root, or would it remain a sinister mystery, and the Young Man thought of the image of himself he so liked, striding like a hero on that June morning into a church where he would slaughter fifteen devout Blacks singing their hymns to God, how with a single masterly blow he would annihilate them, even her, Pastor Anna, and his picture would blaze across every television screen, with his feathered bangs across his forehead, stylish and childlike, his sweater, the boots he'd just bought, they would mention his youth in scandalized tones, he was so young, and later his father would say I do not recognize him as my son, no, it's not him, the suffering of his parents was unfathomable because no, this was not the child they raised, not the child they'd driven to school every morning when he was small, no, it wasn't him, it was someone else,

a stranger, not their son, no, that Young Man with his feathered bangs, cute, mean, hateful, what had he been doing
all that time in the basement, working hard, he said, and
Daniel thought of Mélanie and Mai sailing through the
islands of peace, nudged along by a warm breeze and bask-
ing in the glistering of the light over an ocean so calm in
those peaceful days of June, there were no hurricanes on
the horizon yet, they were nearing the shore where the sea
turtles lazed on golden rocks and on untroubled June mornings white herons and egrets flew lazily by the boats, and
putting aside his interminable book *Strange Years* Daniel
would head out in his Jeep to the archipelago with his kayak
on the roof, alone or with Mai, and as Mai and Mélanie were
doing today he went out on the water, paddled out to the
peaceful islands, an open course beneath the sky where he
and a few others might find a secret verdant paradise among
the ponds, swamps, and sea, and he manoeuvred his kayak
through the mangroves, the pines, the palm trees with their
branches blurred in the wind, he would go have lunch with
a friend, his photographer friend Rémi who lived with his
wife and son in one of the simple houses perched out over
the water, like a fishermen's hut, the ocean literally at their
doorstep and their small boats tied up at the docks, Daniel
followed the path alongside the docks in his kayak beneath
the chirping, looping birds and out came Rémi, who had
decided never to live in the city again, more than that, he
said, he'd quit his profession as a globetrotting journalist
and found refuge with his family in a tropical landscape
where deer and white rabbits ran in the grass, and here, he
said, I am at home, no one is allowed to hunt these gentle
beasts, we live here like humble fishers, and as I told you,
Daniel, at night, between the fishing and the silence of the

waters everything is peaceful, I was exhausted reporting on war after war, seeing women and children dying around me, I've never liked war, you know, I think about them often, Charles and Frédéric, Caroline, Jean-Mathieu, everyone I photographed, I can't believe that they're no longer with us, Daniel, dear Daniel, were we their last witnesses, the last to have approached them, to have known them, they who knew so little about themselves, all they shared was their work, and what do we really learn about them even from their books and paintings and photographs beyond their struggle for integrity as artists in a world that offers such scant support to creators, time and again I imagine Charles and Frédéric, I can see them at the piano rehearsing a Bach sonata together, it's a recurring dream I have at dawn, I can hear the notes and then wake up thinking they haven't really left us, they're still so close, come, my dear Daniel, my wife is looking forward to seeing you, the table is ready outside in the sun, it's not too hot yet, really there's only one thing that disappoints me, or rather my wife and me, we're disappointed by our son, he's in the Middle East at the moment, he joined the army and we can't do a thing about it, Rémi said, taking Daniel's arm, because nothing on this earth belongs to us and to believe the contrary is an illusion, come, my friend, our children's choices aren't always ours, Daniel answered, and then he fell silent, unable to speak Augustino's name, his son who all at once seemed as much a traitor as Rémi's, taking up arms, yet fighting is a courageous thing too, Rémi said, much as it saddens me I do not doubt my son will be a brave soldier but for some time we haven't had any news, none, why is he ignoring us, why doesn't he write to his parents, Rémi asked, or has something happened and we're not being told, we live in fear, Rémi's mother and I, and around five o'clock in the evening Daniel was heading back, thinking of Augustino and of Rémi's son, what heartbreak, he thought, we give our children life and they take it from us twenty years on, why is that, his face was sunburnt and Rémi's words buzzed in his ears as he drove into the blazing five-o'clock summer sky, the roosters and hens cackling, their cries piercing and desperate, they were gathering before nightfall to flutter toward the palm trees that lined the streets and their rising call tore Daniel's soul apart as Rémi's words had done, Rémi repeating, if we had known what they would become and what pain they would cause us, would we have had children, Daniel, you've thought the same thing too haven't you, and the Young Man's parents looked at their son, cuffs on his wrists, the father and mother wondering what lurked behind that imperturbable face, that insolent mouth agape and revealing ferocious teeth, who is that, is he the son of racist slave-owning ancestors or our own son, in whom we inculcated basic moral principles, love your neighbour, do not kill, does it come from his great-grandparents, whose sordid past we know, our son wasn't a member of any party, he wasn't involved in a gang, we thought our son was well behaved, uncommonly well behaved compared to what you hear about kids today, we can confirm that he didn't take drugs, and hardly any alcohol, he's always been a bit vain, that's it, obsessed with hunting, perhaps, an ardent hunter, yes, he liked the smell of the woods, it could be he developed a taste for blood then, he sometimes went hunting for several days in the fall, he would come home completely wired and immediately head down to the basement, intoxicated with, well, we don't want to think about it, yes, little by little hunting made him a murderer, because it was only a sport but the Young Man had told his parents in a brazen outburst that it had also been a sport to kill everybody in the church, a sport like any other, I dreamed of this for a long time and knew that one day my mission would be accomplished, my mission to liberate the whites, because if we do not kill them they will kill us, killing your enemies is justified, it's permitted and they are the enemies of my race, they are your enemies, Father, Momma, you've always refused to see the truth, repeating that we have to get along, be tolerant, even of them, and then on one of those June mornings when a grey light shone through the bars of his cell a man appeared, he came and stood in front of the Young Man with the psychologist, a foreigner, Hispanic, I will be your lawyer, the man said, I'm going to ask that you be transferred from maximum security to another institution for juvenile delinquents, and when the Young Man saw the man who would plead his case he thought, oh, somebody else I don't want to see, somebody else who's despicable, and he winced, he knew that no lawyer, not even this one, could have him moved to juvenile detention, his crimes were those of a fully cognizant adult, calculated and pre-meditated, I don't need you to defend me, he told the lawyer, who felt an inexplicable pity for this child, I'm on the edge of death row, hard by the hallway that leads to the execution chamber, and when the time comes I will plead guilty and I shall die a martyr, a hero for my cause, go away, don't bother with me, who sent you here, have you read my manifesto, don't you know what I think of you, I am here to defend you, the Young Man's lawyer replied calmly, the psychologist and I, and we will do everything we can to help you, because I believe that you're overwhelmed by your crimes, yes, overwhelmed, you had mental issues when you committed them, that's what I'll say in your defence, now listen to me, stop making faces, we'll save you in spite yourself if we have to, whatever ugliness is in you, it shows on your face, it must be addressed, and in time we will address it, though you'll be in a psychiatric institution, you've lost your freedom forever, listen to me, stop making faces, it's not me you're insulting but yourself, and during those same summer evenings, Daniel visited Stephen beneath the acacia arbour, Stephen who was still living at Charles and Frédéric's house, the house Rémi had photographed innumerable times and the garden with the mirror that seemed to reflect Frédéric's large body as he smoked one cigarette after another, in his white slacks, his open shirt revealing his tanned chest, Stephen saying you can see Frédéric is still there, my protector, it was under his complacent eye, not Charles's, he was too strict, that I wrote my book on Eli, I only just sent it in to the publisher, but it's troubling, Stephen said to Daniel, all the more so because the title of my book is *Demons*, and if Eli is a diabolical figure, my own personal demon, then I have to admit it takes two and that the second demon was my love for him, a fantasy, misguided, a mistake that's mine and mine alone, my weakness, I was seduced by a devil with innocent blue eyes but it's my fault, that was my weakness, Stephen said, Eli is locked up where he should be but he haunts me, his threats, I figure he'll be in jail for a few years yet because even in prison he's intractable, he's still trafficking, and he said that as soon as he's out he'll come after me, I no longer see him, I don't visit him in prison anymore, I want the memory of him to fade away but how is that even possible when he's become the main character of a book on crime, I'm exploiting him, he said, and he will have his revenge, my dear

Daniel, how do you manage to write in any kind of peace, you told me that you used to always have a child on your lap, I'd like to meet a man who is simple and good, not particularly handsome, but someone I can trust, and Daniel listened to Stephen beneath the acacias, the petals seemed to fan around Stephen's head like a crown, the air in June always so sweet and fragrant, I have no doubt that you'll find him, said Daniel, he may even be in your life already, Stephen confessed that he had met José, a young cook who'd served him vegetarian dishes in a hotel because Stephen while he was writing didn't eat much but he did drink wine and José wanted to set him right, José wasn't a boy like the others, he was a cook, a humanitarian, at night he drove out in his truck to feed his exquisite dishes to the homeless, he was a boy of admirable charity, Stephen said, but he's incapable of recognizing his own qualities, he's a rare one, could be he's too good and innocent for me but I admire him, literature is beyond him but it doesn't matter, I feel so good with him, he isn't complicated and tortured like me, wouldn't it be a blessing to have him with me day and night, I'd like to marry him but that would be self-serving, as if I didn't have enough strength to be alone after living with a demon, what surrender it is to slip into the embrace of such a kind man, Daniel, shouldn't a writer's experience encompass these contradictions, what do you think, but Daniel was silent, thinking back to Eli the predator offering cocaine to Black children at the pool, in front of the school, Eli the demon Stephen had loved so much, you are not cured, my dear Stephen, but what courage you have to love again, it strikes me as remarkable after such a descent into humiliation and betrayal, betrayal most of all, Stephen said, the worst thing for a man is betrayal but José truly loves me and he's devoted, I could marry him, have a safe, straightforward marriage, the only people he loves more than me are the poor, he brings them meals every night and after driving the length and breadth of the island to feed them he comes to sleep next to me, isn't that what you'd call happiness, Daniel, I shouldn't hesitate, isn't it, and then Stephen was talking about his book with the same passion, with one hand he shooed away the mosquitoes, he had always hated the excesses of tropical nature, the mosquitoes and scorpions and snakes, no, he said, how Charles and Frédéric could have lived in such discomfort escapes me, the insects and reptiles, and Daniel listened, thinking of Frédéric and Charles, it seemed notes were rising up from the piano, that the two were there playing together, Frédéric and Charles, Stephen's voice died out gently as evening fell and when Daniel went back to his house the stars were shining, the air was warmer, after a quick swim in the pool, which was beside the tiny house where Mère had lived with her daughter Mélanie and her grandchildren for so long, beneath the bougainvillea and the garden where Mère had planted flowers with Augustino when he was a child, Daniel rifled through his past and then returned to his office thinking he would write late into the night, the trill of the cicadas breaking the silence, he's still here, Petites Cendres said, the acrobat with the tall red boots, he's walking behind us, tell your parrot not to spread its wings like that, but he's curious, Mabel said, he wants to see what's happening on the beach, is it true that the acrobat leaps through flaming hoops every night, Robbie asked, that guy's not afraid of fire, fire or death, all it takes is one spark and the whole thing goes up, he can't help it, it's his livelihood, Mabel said, like me and Jerry, we are all of us continually

exposed to the cruelty of men, that's how they killed my
Merlin, and if it was God's will why am I a devout woman,
why, eh, Mabel said, her waving arm jostling the parrot
perched on her hand, wings wide open, there you go, Mabel
said to her parrot, you're obedient, you grip the fingers of
my right hand like I taught you, don't forget that I'm carrying a very heavy bag, the walk will be long yet, come back
to my shoulder, Jerry, do what I taught you, especially
because he's wearing lace silk shorts, Robbie laughed, and
a red shirt over top, for him, for that cross-dressing acrobat,
it's the senses that are most provocative, passersby stick to
his skin and they're burned by his fire, the acrobatics of
foolish desire, it reminds me of when I was with Old Daddy,
people used to stick to my skin like that when we travelled
together, they wanted to know what brought us together,
Old Daddy and me, sex of course, I always answered, sex,
on my shoulder I had a tattoo that said I belonged to Daddy,
we were on the beach in San Diego, some kids were training for the Olympics and others were surfing the ocean
waves or practising yoga on the sand, those were good
times, when I was young enough to please him, I ended
my career with him, some time afterwards I went back to
the ocean, to the beach in San Diego when others were
surfing high on the cresting waves, yeah, it was with Fatalité,
when she was so skinny but trying to be healthy, she would
look out at the ocean, at the sky, barely able to see, quietly
undone by blindness and the ravages of the disease, I was
there, standing with her in the wind and she said in that
voice that wasn't hers anymore will you remember us, will
you remember me, that I'm the prettiest of the girls and that
I can dance better than anyone else on a cabaret stage, tell
Yinn to leave a light on in my room, in the evening, let there

be a light in the night, no darkness for a month, when that
last evening comes I'll do what I do every night, around
four in the morning I'll cross the street in my high heels, I'll
be wearing the blond wig with the red highlights, my walk
will be weary, I'll barely be able to stand, the club with the
red neon lights is right in front of my apartment so I'll head
up the stairs to my apartment in my own slow, unexpected
way and the light will shine on in my room and the needle,
the beguiling poison, my overdose will be there, yeah, you
hear what I'm saying, don't you Robbie, so why are you
being so weird all of a sudden, this place, San Diego, I told
Fatalité, is the capital of health, don't think about anything
anymore, Fatalité, listen to the wind, the waves, listen, forget
what's going to happen, Fatalité, forget, I was soothing
Fatalité with my words as if to put a crying child to sleep
and one year later it was Herman we'd be comforting, it's
like a black flower on your leg, we'd say, after the operation
everything will be better, Herman, come dance, sing, he
was off to Mexico and Provincetown for the last shows, his
mother, his sisters would come along for the day, and then
his light was snuffed out, we had put him in a room rented
near Yinn's, close to us, his devastated, capitulating queens,
relinquishing, tell us, Yinn repeated, you're not high, we
know you, you're always high, why wouldn't you be high
now, it was his mother who closed his eyes, bravely she
said boys you know I love you as I loved him, Herman, it's
a joy for a mother to have such a whimsical child, I love
you all, no sobs or anything, then she drew her fingers over
Herman's eyes, staring out into space, that's how it was,
Robbie said to Petites Cendres, there are babies on the boat
with them too, I see them reaching out their hands to us,
Mabel said, and no one's coming, there they are with their

mothers bent over the waves and at night the water will wash over them and tomorrow on the beach we'll see what bodies the sea gives up, I see only the yachts, Robbie said, what are you on about now, Mabel, the regatta is in a few days, Robbie said, Reverend Ézéchielle paid for my plane ticket so that I could go and see my daughter, Mabel said, she had her fourth baby and I was thinking as I held the little one on my lap, pretty boy child, I thought what will become of you, will a white policeman put a bullet in your back while you're playing with toy guns in the park, smart-ass that you'll turn out to be, beckoning them over with your toy guns, pretty child, why be born if only to be attacked when you're older, eh, Mabel whispered, as if she were singing in the warm breeze, he's my daughter's fourth child, my daughter lives so far away but Reverend Ézéchielle didn't forget me, she said, go, go at this moment of joy, Mabel, go and worship the glory of the Lord, his name shall be Glory, I was thinking, I'd like him to be named Glory in honour of his Creator, but will there even be a future, Robbie says that even Black policemen are killing Black children and that no one is paying them any mind, theirs will be a lost generation, but my daughter will have a fifth child and a sixth, life must go on, Mabel said, I was from a lost generation too, Robbie said, and look, we have to defend ourselves but we're still here, lost generations make the best survivors, Robbie said, that's what you can't see, Mabel, you and your prayers, those whose destiny it is to be lost blossoms like buds on the trees, that's what you don't know, Mabel, Robbie said, and Petites Cendres was listening but acutely aware of the presence of the men and women around them wearing shark masks and the acrobat in the red boots and skimpy getup went down to the beach with

his hoops for the fire show, and later that night beneath the
blue edge of the sky he would say it again, he was fireproof,
and in his cell the Young Man was contemplating the prison's
avenues, the halls he walked along during the day between
two giants who never stopped watching over him even
though he was handcuffed, his wrists bound, their eyes
pierced him like knives, and the racket of the mob of prisoners screaming as he passed, hey, we'll rape you, you'll
get what's coming to you, wait until nightfall, wait until you
go to the showers, just wait, we're gonna rape you, every
one of us, and he shuddered with fear when he heard the
words, the men shouting, he wasn't sure what race they
were but he was terrified, his white body was so clean, he
would be violated relentlessly, no respect for his modesty,
he knew how vicious they were, how sadistic, the white
supremacist and Hispanic gangs, and he thought about the
white skin he washed every day, he looked like a virgin
girl, one voice had shouted we're going to make a man out
of him, a real one, we're going to show him the games men
play, and most of all he heard their vulgar, suggestive laughter and he thought about the joggers, the joggers in the
parks, in the public gardens of Charleston, the girls in his
class at school who mocked him, who said he was white
as snow, he could see them now, two of them, killed in the
church and lying at his feet and their hair under the soles
of his boots, ha, white as snow, was that it, yes, he got them
good, their jeers, their Black-girl taunts, he'd punished them,
bang, bang, like those men yelling their barbaric desires
when they saw him being marched around between the
two guards, head held high but his face so pale, how many
times he'd thought of snagging one of the joggers and
making her pay for his lust, for wanting her, her skin

shining in the sun, he wanted to bite her, to know the taste of her thick lips, and she would pay, rape, he would wait until the end of the day, watching, waiting, then grab her by the neck and throw her down onto the rough grass and afterwards he would slink away, not touching her even though he knew how it would go, it would be so easy for him, he'd learned early in his hunts how to handle game, how to finish off his prey, but panting with desire, with guilt, he didn't move, he hid in the grove, breathing hard, the girl with the splendid black legs, black under the white skirt of her school uniform, it made his head spin, crushed him, her power was insurmountable, even though she was inches from him he froze, though nothing in the world would have been easier he didn't dare, he did nothing, no, the word rape gripped him when they were so close in the gym or jogging at the end of the day, they were faster than he was, and more agile, but it would have been so easy, grabbing an arm, a leg, but it was better to have them in his sights, this time in the church as they prayed he wouldn't miss, and no longer would they say look, here's whitey, white as white cloth, his skin the colour of snow, no, they wouldn't dare make fun of him anymore, he would put an end to the ripples of laughter as they ran together, meanwhile those bastards in the prison want to rape me up against a wall, rape me, but no one can come near me, not even my mother, I'm untouchable, skin the colour of chalk the girls said, running, flaunting their legs in front of him, they were so supple, desirable, he was stricken, yes, you, in the degradation of your desire, your base sexual appetites, you will give in, come play with the boys, the men shouted from their cells, their hands clutching the bars, faceless, they were yelling, they screamed yes, you'll be initiated like all the others, hah, you're so cocky, so proud, and the psychologist asked the Young Man, these young girls, you knew them, didn't you, and you callously wiped them out, yet they seemed to be your friends, your classmates, what do feelings have to do with it, the Young Man replied, was I supposed to have feelings, but remember, you broke them, you killed them, it's a horrible story, how will you explain it to your lawyer, so awful, the psychologist said, you went jogging with these girls and the Young Man said it again, robotically, in a monotone voice, they laughed at me, in class, jogging in the park, they laughed at me, and looking down at his handcuffed wrists the Young Man said no one can make fun of me, and as he walked along other hallways, other wings of the prison, breathing in the smell of the rutting men who wanted him, of the mouldy walls and stone stairs, the Young Man shook with fear, those eyes looking his way, all those hands stretching their fingers through the bars, they wanted to desecrate him, or was he dirty already, he was, wasn't he, he who was always so clean, so neat, no one had ever touched him or caressed him or was he dreaming, was this how the nightmare went, on and on, yes, was it too late, and her smile in the church kept coming back to him, intent on calming his furious, battering heart, Pastor Anna smiling and, in her agony, asking why don't you go home to your parents, why don't you go home, and the twelve-year-old suicide bomber would kill no one today, no bus would be blown up in the city centre, she had fled to the purple hills and to the other side of a barbed-wire fence where her parents and brothers and sisters were waiting, the passing minutes and seconds sounding the alarm, bombs dangling like bells around her waist, she looked like a goat scrambling up the rocks, were those braids or an

animal's tail, her hair flying behind her in the wind, her hair
uncovered, which should have been the end of her, and the
deaths of thirty strangers too, better to mistake her for a
rough-haired goat galloping to the hills, and soon the sun
would set on the purple mountain, her thin silhouette melting into the fading light, and the minutes and seconds would
ring her reprieve, she would meet a man who would relieve
her of the suicide belt, who would speak to her kindly, go
my child to join your family, this way, over there, I will take
you there in my cart, see, there's my donkey, he'll lead us
there slower than slow but that's the pace of the donkey
labouring on our behalf, for humankind, and see, it'll be
night soon, a girl shouldn't be alone in these fields at the
foot of the purple mountain, you see we are at war today
as we were yesterday, my girl, listen to me, I had to bury a
daughter who was about your age, let me help you, that
belt around your waist, what is it, tell me, where did you
come from running like that, where do you come from and
what is your name, I had a child, a few months ago she was
still with us, I had a daughter who looked like you, and the
girl ran toward the trees in the wind, the leafy trees on the
purple hillside, and behind the barbed wire of the camp
her parents and her sisters were waiting, her belt dangled
and clanged, bearded men with their faces covered had told
her, go, you are our messenger, go, in the city there's a
market where they sell spices and nearby is a bus, listen
carefully, you are our messenger, they are the target, you
won't feel a thing, you won't have time, or she hadn't been
told a thing, she'd heard the men's laughter as they girded
her frail waist with the string of explosive bells, quickly, go,
it's almost time, you'll recognize the market, it's where they
sell spices, lots of women will be there, but the girl had

decided not to side with the enemy, no longer would she be raped and radicalized, no, today no woman or child would be killed at the market because of her, and in the moment how she wanted to protect them, other young girls were heading to Syria and their parents would search for them forever because they had new identities, where was the man who would say to her come, I'll take you to the refugee camp where your parents are waiting, the purple mountain stood so high in the mist and what if a plume of white smoke was trailing her as she ran, ran, what if one of the little bombs had burst and she hadn't even noticed, her flesh such insubstantial fabric, and as the twelve-year-old suicide bomber stumbled toward the purple mountain she kept thinking, today I will not get onto that bus crowded with mothers and their children wailing with hunger, I will not, no, they will not die because of me, those mothers will live to nurse their children once more, and without fear, tonight and tomorrow these mothers and children will live, haven't they lost fathers, uncles, cousins, brothers, isn't that enough, two hundred and twenty thousand dead, refugees in the millions, isn't that enough, and among the detained there are masses of minors, the suicide bombers of tomorrow, farewell to the traitors and dictators who forced my parents into exile, who split them up, some of my country's survivors brought no more than a piece of stone from home, they hold it in their hands, farewell to fields of ruins, or a pebble, what was left of their bombed-out home, only a pebble, I want to see my mother, the twelve-year-old girl thought, will I recognize her in the camp, my mother, a young woman hiding her face under a black veil, whose brother was shot in Yarmouk by one of the fighters of this despicable insurgency, but now the alarm was going off on

her belt and the twelve-year-old suicide bomber's heart was
beating louder, where is the path to the refugee camp and
where is he, wasn't that him, the man with his cart coming
closer to her now, wasn't that him coming out of the woods
with his donkey, the animal looked like it was sleeping, and
as he pushed his cart ahead he said keep going, the camp
is very far from here, we'll get rid of that belt in the river,
aren't you a bit afraid, girl, aren't you, what's the use of
assigning the death of others to you, you're only a child, I
had a daughter who looked like you, no, thought the girl
suicide bomber, I won't be on that bus crowded with women
and children tonight, and every bell on the twelve-year-old's
belt sounded the alarm, I will not kill anyone, not on the
bus and not at the market with its fruit and vegetable stands,
no, not tonight and not tomorrow, so the mothers can feel
milk fill their breasts and not be afraid, they are at the back
of crowded buses, they have lost a brother, a sister, or a
child too, their son only recently born or their oldest daughter, soon the light of the setting sun will fade against the
purple hills, against a man and his cart, a donkey that seems
to be dozing along the roads, oh, I will find them, my parents, tonight or tomorrow, in the camp behind the barbed
wire, yes, I will manage to find them, thought the twelve-
year-old suicide bomber, and otherwise my body, so thin
already, will implode, but it will be the implosion of the sun
between my ribs, otherwise, otherwise I can't think about
what's going to happen, I've been walking for so long that
every single thought makes me dizzy, I have to find my
parents as soon as I can, and Suzannah hesitated, she was
thirteen, Suzannah, humiliated by her father on the internet,
had she seen those videos, the father cutting his daughter's
hair to punish her for her recklessness, for texting and

sending videos to boys, who hadn't seen the staged shaming, a father formally humiliating his daughter in front of
countless invisible spectators in the pellucid theatre of the
internet, where any aggression can be broadcast, it's quite
a lesson from modern parents, parents no longer whip their
offspring, this is trendier, and more public, parents making
videos in which they play the role of right-minded educa-
tors, and for the children the humiliation is so much a part
of their lives that they sometimes join in, I'm worthless, I
know it, my parents said so and I believe it, Father, I apolo-
gize for misplacing my iPad, I'm worthless, yes, I know it,
I'm always the worst student in my class and I know my
future will be miserable, Suzannah had seen these videos,
her father had shown them to her and she knew one day
she would be punished too, outrageously, for how bold she
was with boys, she was always writing to them, she was so
attractive at thirteen, she sent pictures of herself in a bikini
to one of them for fun, to excite them though it didn't actually mean anything, as she told her friends, I'm young, I'm
so young, I have my whole life ahead of me, thirteen-year-
old Suzannah stood on the edge of the highway and hesitated for a moment, a butterfly with yellow and brown wings
landed on her shoulder and flitted around her shorn head,
then on her arm, as if to say to her, no, no, don't do it, the
butterfly's beauty made her hesitate and the humiliation
hurt a little less right then, it was a sunny day in June and
the cars zooming down the highway were carrying young
holiday-makers, lovers, postcard landscapes stretching before
them, landscapes she would never have the time to know
because none of them, not one of these people, not one of
these passengers or travellers, had been publicly humiliated
and savaged by their fathers on YouTube like she had been,

not one, no, not even the children who were drawing in
the air with their fingers through the car window, tracing
greetings, hello, hello, how are you, they shouted, she
couldn't help but see the mortifying video over and over,
she was lying on the living room carpet, the unsightly mop
of blond hair her father had chopped off lying in front of
her, but because she had her back turned you couldn't see
her face, she thought no one could see anything, only a
shamed child twisted on the floor, her shame invisible to
the eye, imperceptible, her father had called it a public
shaming so that she wouldn't do it again, we tried everything
and you never seemed to understand but this time, yes, you
will be so humiliated that you will understand, decency
through technology, there's nothing else your mother and
I can do because you never listen to us, you and your
friends, your generation doesn't listen to anyone, you're all
ego and we're at wits' end, I can find no discipline that
works but this one I think speaks your language, the games
you play, sending each other videos, this one will suit you,
and so her hair was torn and sheared, the father was the
executioner of her hair, it was the worst punishment for
Suzannah, she was outraged, but she was powerless, she
couldn't see her friends, her classmates, she thought, without
her luxurious hair, her crowning glory, you see, her father
said, there's nothing now, are you so attractive now, no,
look at yourself and repeat after me, I behaved terribly with
my father, he corrected me and he was right, I know I
haven't got a chance, I'll end up in reform school when I
grow up, except that Suzannah had not been able to speak
the words in front of her father, she fled, quickly she was
in the street, like an arrow she dashed into the dusty shadows of the highway, cars, trucks, she was about to throw

herself under one of the trucks, they smelled like oil, when the butterfly with the brown and yellow wings landed on her shoulder, whirling, fluttering to her arm, to her hand open in the thick June air, it was exhilarating, the butterfly turning and flurrying as if it were breathing, almost inaudibly, not yet, not yet, your mother is coming, she's always stood up for you, she's on her way, she'll be here soon, she'll take you in her arms gasping for breath and tell you let's go, let's find somewhere else to live without him, I can't take it any more, my children are bullied by their father, my beloved children bullied and persecuted, it's unbearable, we'll leave together, you and me, we'll live somewhere else without him from now on, oh, my long-haired daughter, what did he do to you, you were down on your knees crying over your hair, my child, humiliated, and to him that's what educating our children is about, even barbers try to resist harsh, punitive parents, they give boys a buzz cut but they say we don't like it, we have to tell the parents that's how old men cut their hair, it's an old-man haircut, no, that's mean, why would you treat your children like that, they are only borrowed from God, why do you choose to harm them, we barbers don't like to see these little-old-man heads, isn't this imposing an inexpressible indignity on them, and Suzannah thought, if her mother came, yes, we could go somewhere else together, the wide world, does my mother fear him, my mother with her blond hair, my father runs his hand through it, does she fear him as much as I do, she says he's your father, you have to listen to him, obey him, the hand of brute violence, he's my father, yes, and wasn't that her, her mother, running along the highway, sweating in the dust, Mama, Mama, Suzannah shouted, if you don't come now I'll be crushed under the wheels, I'm so ashamed Mama,

and the yellow and brown butterfly was fluttering, wait, a
woman shouted, wait, forget those videos, so much nasti-
ness, wait, Suzannah, can't you see I'm coming to you, we'll
leave, enough of this house where my children are abused
and persecuted, I can't take it anymore, I wanted to tell you
sooner but I've always felt such dread around him, that he
would cut us off, deprive us of everything, you and your
brothers and sisters, yes, was that her mother on the horizon,
she would come, Suzannah thought, she would come, there
were so many animals on the side of the highway, insignificant creatures, birds, rabbits, and squirrels of the flayed
forests sacrificed, Suzannah would slip into a coffin of fur
and broken bones, she would, she thought, without anyone
noticing and under the blue sky all the shame would fade,
who would remember her if her mother didn't come, though
heaven in its unconditional mercy accepts every gift, every
offering, and now the moment at which an innocent child
would be sucked below the wheels of a truck was close,
the yellow-brown-winged butterfly continued its dance, no,
listen to me, your mother is coming, it seemed to whisper
in Suzannah's ear, why won't you listen, the agony of death
is greater than you believe, it's unconscionable, even if it's
instantaneous you won't be able to bear the pain and you
will have left me, the yellow and brown butterfly whispered,
you'll have left me, and Suzannah knew at that moment that
out of the tomb of the highway where her soul would rest,
her small body rent into a thousand pieces like the rabbit,
the bird, the squirrel, her fellow martyrs, out of her death
would come a law, a law championed by an association of
young lawyers campaigning for social justice, a law to punish
parents whose punishment of their children is criminal,
parents who humiliate their children online, no longer would

the trolling eyes of the internet delight in the shaming, complicit, and when Suzannah's mother found her child on the highway, pulling over in her car, it was already too late, too late, and a few days later, between two off-ramps on the highway to Illinois, Suzannah's mother, her brothers, her sisters would lay flowers and toys, teddy bears and dolls, in front of a cross planted in a patch of greenery with the words *we are thinking of you Suzannah, we'll never forget you Suzannah*, and as she walked ever so slowly singing by the sea, Mabel admonished her parrot, Jerry, don't be hopping from one leg to the other like that on my shoulder, she said, you're pecking at my neck, my old neck, wrenched by my years, I'm telling you, especially those years when I was almost penniless working for whites, and she said to Robbie with a melancholy tone, the hot air making her reedy voice tremble, I remember that when the end came the little one was still asking to see his father, the monster never even came to see his son, but he will pay, the wretch, because you pay for everything, you young people don't know that, Eureka would come by in the evening after her choir rehearsals and ask Angel, feverish and restless in his bed, how do you feel my darling, do you want me to rub your chest, no, it's like the tide, it rises and falls, Angel murmured, the ache is like the tide, it's a wave that comes and goes, go to sleep and don't think about it anymore, Eureka said, placing a damp cloth on Angel's forehead and caressing his hair with her wet hand, Angel, there's nothing more beautiful than the sea and the tide rising and receding and the waves, listen, but oh you can't hear them because your mother closed the window, let's open everything up, Eureka exclaimed, and with her thick arms she threw the bedroom window open, enough with the fans, she said, better to let the air and the sound of the sea and the song of the egrets flow in, they fly so fast, it comes and goes, Angel repeated, it's a peculiar discomfort, not too painful but it comes and goes and keeps me from sleeping, the doctor said no humid air, the sea is humid, Angel said, I'd like us to take off in a boat, yeah, in Joë's sailboat, with Brilliant, where's Brilliant, he'll come later, Eureka said, and she rocked him, reassured him, her baby, she'd always made fun of his long legs, how fast he was growing, she teased him, gripped by a sharp pang of what he called his discomfort, Angel asked Eureka there will be singing, right, Daddy says he doesn't want singing but Mama says there will be lots of singing, they're not the same religion, one is atheist and the other Catholic, they never got along, but songs, we need songs, and Angel would end up falling asleep with Misha against him, big fat Misha, and Mabel promised more than songs, a whole choir, the Black Ancestral Choir and the women's voices like the sounds of flutes, yes, but the men, strong voices, too strong, and in the shack by the sea Eureka asked Angel, who will notice the tenors eh, voices to make the earth tremble, yes, I'm telling you, you know, Angel, you look like Jesus, do you know what He did, He was able to raise Himself from the dead, and you can too, you can feel better right now, yes, I'm telling you, Angel, you can do like Jesus, and where's Kitty, when is she coming, we were supposed to play together this morning, Angel said, looking to the window, the sea on the other side of Atlantic Boulevard, even though she's back at school Kitty comes to play with me every day, in the city, she's so happy, she's studying math in the end, Angel whispered, Kitty, where's Kitty, Angel asked, when he started staring off into nothing like it was Mars he was looking for, yeah, he said, we could be there soon, that wandering star, young astronauts sign lifetime contracts to explore the infinite, limitless territory of the heavens and the vastness of the wandering stars, Angel said, the thought lifted her up, Mabel said, because Angel may well have been able to see something we don't and Eureka kept saying you should go to sleep now so you can be strong, there I was with Angel, ginger beer in hand, and he was thanking me for having brought Jerry, what a nice boy, and a convoy was going by and Robbie said to Petites Cendres, hey, Petites Cendres, look, a Black funeral, look at that man in the felt hat playing the trumpet, that ceremonious slowness, the music with its funereal gravity sows the seeds of melancholy in me, it's both lofty and morbid but don't worry, Petites Cendres, today's not your day, you're too jaunty, too defiant, it would be unfortunate if this procession were yours or mine but I think it's for one of those young Black soldiers who won't be coming home from Afghanistan, or rather who was doomed to come home in a pine box, there you go, so many we've stopped counting, Robbie said, they'll have state funerals, Mabel said, this young man might have been as old as one of my sons, it's too bad that all of us, great and small, we are no more than dust and ashes before God, ah, Robbie said, if he's immortal then your god didn't create us in his image, don't you see that you've been lied to, Mabel, you've been carried away by nonsense, if we were in his image there would never be these sad parades, and the clarion of the trumpet, what could be more saddening, more demoralizing, just listening to it I feel like I'm six feet under, oh good, they're moving away, now there's only the sound of water and the cooing of white pigeons on the sand, so that's how it is, Robbie said to Petites Cendres reproachfully, you

didn't tell me anything about your summer flu, you didn't
say a word, as if you no longer trusted your brother, yes,
I'm your brother, Robbie said, or am I your brother, can't
you answer me, Robbie said, but Petites Cendres didn't say
anything, he was distracted by the intrusive figures skulking
behind them, behind their masks they have shark teeth,
they're shouting insults and obscenities, about us it seems,
they're spying on us, one of them said people like you, we
should kick you out, get rid of you, you're degenerates, the
two of you and that old Black woman, trash, trash, the masks
below their straw hats inscrutable, I think they don't like
us, Petites Cendres said to Robbie, who, them, Robbie asked,
laughing sarcastically, them, they're only kids partying,
they're still drunk, don't listen to them, they're only following us because they can't walk by themselves, too many
margaritas all night long, they can hardly walk straight, one
of them has no head, Petites Cendres said, he's their leader,
his head is a red balloon, he's taking off his mask to let us
see the balloon and then putting it back on, he's the one
who's been yelling insults at us, he's wearing a white hood
like the Ku Klux Klan with only two holes for the eyes, but
it's a head without a face, a balloon, it's grotesque, like an
apparition, it's something out of a nightmare Petites Cendres
said, I think I've seen him at the bar and now he's coming
after us, you're imagining things Robbie said, breathe, man,
breathe in the salty sea air my friend, we're walking on
jasmine flowers, we are flooded with their perfume, and in
the scalding gush of the shower the Young Man felt himself
struck down by fear, they would come rape him, there they
were a few steps away he was sure the tattooed men
belonged to white supremacist gangs, their sexuality was
predatory, they were criminals, furtive, white men who'd

killed Blacks while the Young Man was no more than an apprentice criminal, he'd committed crimes, but like a child playing awkwardly with toy guns, he thought, clumsy and foolish, he'd have to start over and do better, he thought, maybe exterminate the girls first, spare Pastor Anna and her persistent smile, yes, he would do it differently, the girls deserved his punishment, they had made fun of him in class, in the gym, everywhere, but Pastor Anna was innocent, go back to your parents she'd said, it's not too late, and the water splashed on the Young Man's face and through the hair over his forehead, he knew that the guard was waiting near the sinks to take him back to his cell and that the other men couldn't come near him, he knew his hands would be bound as soon as he got out of the shower, his wrists, who knows if they weren't taking such good care of him simply to get him ready for the gallows, he was treated with such respect, it was all so exclusive that it could only mean the worst, he thought, and he could hear the gang of white supremacists, their screams through the water, hey, here comes the new guy, a voice shouted, he's running away, they keep him nice and safe, this one, his cell in solitary isn't far, it's right by the mysterious chamber, the room of sanctioned executions, they had no kindness for the Young Man, the shouts and screams amplified by the echoes of the voices echoing in the soapy steamy room, the guard waited as he had been ordered to do, at a distance, waited for the Young Man to finish cleaning up and put on his numbered uniform and he took charge of the Young Man as if he were, according to some unyielding principle of possession, his property, and he steered him toward his final destination, that was why he was being treated better than the other prisoners the Young Man thought, in preparation for the judge's sentence, his fatal words, and when the prison guard went home that night he would tell his wife and children about the Young Man, at the dinner table he would tell them that he was in charge of a prisoner who was going to be sentenced to death, or did he just wolf down his meal in a silence that felt slightly threatening, the guard waited for the Young Man so he could take him back to his cell without any interference from the brawny, full-grown men, the white supremacists who were screaming dementedly in the shower, was he being spared from the tattooed brutes, they didn't dare approach him, his clean, virginal body, was he being spared now only to suffer some unspeakable punishment later like a sword cutting off his head, he would be lying on a wooden bed with a thin white cloth and a pillow, the pillow might be raw silk or of immaculate white cotton and after he had ingested the meal of his choosing, a steak almost raw, a salad, some cake for dessert, you can smoke a cigarette if you want to but not for more than a few seconds, the device would flood him with electricity and he would stumble into nothingness, bang, and he would be buried in a mass grave for executed commoners, a forgotten hero, or would it be the opposite, would the judge say can't you see he's too young, life in prison, and he wouldn't be forgotten, he would be writing his manifestos, because the hatred that consumed him would never run dry, no, never, and in his office bathed in the June sunlight, at once intense and so gentle, Daniel thought of friends he admired because they seemed to live a more serene life, friends who'd been mentors, friends who'd escaped the tyranny of the computer of which Daniel was an unqualified captive, today they wrote letters, handwritten letters on stationery, Jean-Mathieu's calligraphy traced out

with a steel-nib pen, writing to Charles who had retired to
an ashram in India, my friend I am transfixed by your asceti-
cism, I'm writing to you from my terrace overlooking the
sea, why won't you come back to us, what high-minded
purification are you seeking so far away from us, through
hardships I've earned my own room in the heights, when
I was young I crewed a ship in Halifax, and I sailed, became
a writer, I remember the doves, the bald eagles, the hum-
mingbirds, and long ago in my country, sandpipers by the
ponds and the lakes, I recorded the herons' migrations in
my notebook, how they flew, I loved the herons, from
Oregon to the south of Idaho and then from the north to
the West Indies, yes, Jean-Mathieu found the time was right
for meditation, for reflection, from the terrace of his seaside
apartment a poet was able to dream before the setting sun,
the steel pen in his hand hovering over his vellum paper,
Jean-Mathieu worried about leaving for Italy on his own,
without Caroline, he had always travelled with her, though
this wouldn't be the first time, as he wrote to Charles, he
understood Caroline preferred the company of her young
driver to his, an old intellectual perpetually hunched over
his writing, Jean-Mathieu was working on a biography of
Stendhal and it was consuming all of him, his passion,
everything in him lived only for literature, for the arts, and
obviously Jean-Mathieu understood that Caroline would
rather be with the young woman from the West Indies whose
portrait she'd made for a well-received photography exhibition, a young woman who was somewhat intriguing, he
wrote, who seemed to charm Caroline and stimulate her
work, but not everything new is charming, Jean-Mathieu
wrote to Charles, and old age must wrestle with monotony
and with ennui, the enticements of youth are an appeal to

our vanity, first I'll go to Milan, following in Stendhal's footsteps, Jean-Mathieu wrote to Charles, during his stay in Italy
he hadn't yet written *Le Rouge et le Noir*, and Daniel reflected
on the long correspondence between the two poets, the
delighted witticisms they traded with a certain paternalistic
pride, Jean-Mathieu was the oldest of Daniel's poet friends
and he was always giving Charles advice, Charles who was
too isolated in his ashram in India, my friend, but oughtn't
we try to escape despair, at the time it was a bit of a miracle,
given Jean-Mathieu's innocence, thought Daniel, he seemed
unaffected by external life, by the aggravations of politics
and social chaos, he spoke of the superiority of art over
violence, even to the point of being blind or insensitive to
it, Jean-Mathieu was convinced that any major disaster could
be avoided or held at bay if only we knew how to divert
tyrants from their nefarious projects by offering them concerts or readings by their favourite authors, as if a tyrant or
a head of state hell-bent on destroying humanity might be
sensitive to a novel or poem, if he might be a reader or
could actually be moved by a piece of music by even as
magnificent a virtuoso as Paganini, Jean-Mathieu wrote
Charles, could the sound of the violin not overpower the
ear of a madman, making him forget in that second of dis-
traction his intention to annihilate us the next day, daydreaming in front of the ocean, his tanned hand resting on the
letter paper, refusing to see that ignorance was usually the
force behind genocide, ignorance and greed, it seemed to
Daniel that Jean-Mathieu belonged to another time, it took
only one man so ignorant and greedy, narcissistic and perverse, to set off the apparatus of a nuclear war, only that,
Daniel thought, for it to be over, but on that June morning
the baby birds were chirping, chicks in the garden, and

Daniel smiled as he heard the silky peeps, what delicious respite, thought Daniel, the sound of their chirping, he kept trying to lead the hen back to her chicks but she was drawn to the street, her babies trundling under her wing straight to danger, as if the deafening noise of the street made her lose all caution, come, come here to the oleander and the lilies, Easter flowers, hybrids, to Mère's small house where I imagine I can still hear Schubert, you'll be safe here, come, come, Daniel said to the hen and her chicks, relieved to be out of his office, to feel the warmth of the sun on his face, the chirping of the chicks, what he was writing was weighing down his conscience, the discomfort lingered, he knew it was impossible for him to be cured of the distress he felt while he was writing about the Young Man who lived within him now, he never left him alone, the Young Man of whom Daniel had unintentionally become a controversial, questionable judge, who is a lonely writer to judge others, he wondered, didn't the Young Man believe that he wielded the sword of justice, that his crimes, committed with neither remorse nor repentance, were just, he had convinced himself that his victims had to die because they were Black, the delusions white supremacists' minds were made of, abounding, they festered among racists, thought Daniel, the world was populated by demons, fanatics both secular and religious, nothing seemed to be able to prevent their rise and our ruin, and in the crash of the waves Petites Cendres thought he heard Yinn's footsteps as he climbed the stairs to the cabaret, the staircase bathed in a white light, Yinn walked up, resting a hand on Victoire's shoulder and said, come on, everything will go well tonight, it'll be a great show, dear Victoire, why must you always fret, let me free you from your worries, you'll see, Yinn said to Victoire in a suggestive whisper, Victoire was always so dourly dressed even if she was going to be dancing all night, even in flats she was too tall, while Yinn, Petites Cendres remembered, Yinn who had changed his persona some time ago, perched high up on stilettos, daintily wiggling his hips in a very short black dress, a pearl necklace around his neck and, much to Petites Cendres' displeasure, his hair cut in the latest fashion, it would have suited a monk better than Yinn, whose hair had once cascaded down to his shoulders, Yinn's hair or lack thereof, the trendy hairstyle his husband Jason also sported, his head was adorned with an Afro wig, curls and dreads tumbling over Yinn's forehead and, noticing Petites Cendres hesitating at the bottom of the stairs, his cheeks were pale, was he hesitating or still too smitten with Yinn, he would have leapt up the staircase in a single bound to join Yinn up there but no, he was still punishing himself for loving him too much, Petites Cendres hadn't seen Yinn for months, when Yinn saw that Petites Cendres seemed troubled or distant he shouted, hey, Petites Cendres, come to the show tonight, you won't regret it, it's gonna be sexy, not because of our Victoire here, she's always a bit embarrassed by our flamboyance, that's what we're here for, isn't it, flamboyance, but because the Louisiana Diva is our guest tonight, you have to come and cheer her on, Petites Cendres, come by, my darling friend, and those words, darling friend, whipped up Petites Cendres' simmering passion for Yinn, he felt desire course through his body, and where have you been, Yinn said, we've hardly seen you at the cabaret, you used to be here every night, Yinn repeated, where were you, at the Acacia Gardens, Yinn, I was at the Acacia Gardens where life is comfortable, Petites Cendres said, I'm there because of you, Yinn, don't think I don't know it, but,

suddenly shy, Petites Cendres bit back these words of troubled gratitude, he followed Yinn and Victoire to the stage,
sitting at the bar by the ladder Jason would soon pull over
to the lighting booth and Petites Cendres thought, here I
am, I'm back, back with Yinn, who is so exquisite, a gift,
my all-too-human frailty, divine, my treasure that anyone
can break but who'll never be mine, because Yinn was
married to Jason, and as Petites Cendres mooned over the
one he loved, his adoration for Yinn revived, a group of
young men trundled up the stairs, they were very drunk
and as they rushed to the bar in peals of boorish laughter,
they were lampooning Petites Cendres and the queens,
lame, they said, dancing on the stage they mocked the drag
queens, ha ha, weren't they hilarious in their getups, Petites
Cendres bristled at their derision, their insults, and he would
have kicked the lot of them down the stairs and into the
street but Robbie said discreetly, no, you can't, Yinn wouldn't
like it, the coarse vulgarity of the insults they'd hurled at
Yinn burned him up, and now as he walked along the beach
it seemed like the waves were rising and Yinn's splendid
figure vanished into the water along with the young men's
mockery, their taunts, their silent hatred and his inability to
defend himself but Robbie shook him as they walked, what's
wrong, where did you go there, you're lost in thought,
brother, I'm telling you that if we don't rise up against this
unholy law in North Carolina we won't even be able to
relieve ourselves in public restrooms without having to show
our birth certificate, I'm not thinking about me or you, off-
stage we're men, I'm thinking about the young transgender
kids, about Victoire, what'll happen to Victoire and the kids
who've reclaimed their true selves, the gender that is theirs
but which they lost through some accident of biology, what

do you say, Petites Cendres, like you I think the law is inhuman and depraved, Petites Cendres said, but all he could think of was Yinn dancing on the stage as the audience jeered, so nasty, using their smartphones to distort Yinn's picture on their screens, you're not hearing me Robbie said, you'd rather Victoire was humiliated, you'd rather she be forced to undress or have to take her birth certificate out of her purse, isn't that discrimination at its most cowardly, yes, of course I believe that, absolutely, Petites Cendres said, look, we're getting closer to Pelican Beach, Mabel said, a bit closer with every step, can't we sit down and drink some water, my legs are killing me, Mabel said, this bag is so heavy, Lena told me she would bring Misha even though he's heartbroken, Lena said she'll bring Misha, and you, my poor Jerry, you must be thirsty too, but seeing Misha laughing on the beach will do me good, they used to come to the beach together all the time when the boy was able to swim, yes, to swim, like any other child, while his mother read a book on the beach, you know, Robbie, there's always a governor who'll stand up against such a law, Petites Cendres said to Robbie, men are not all bad, there's always someone who resists, who says no, we must not, no, only we can stop this Robbie said, you and me, Yinn and the girls, us, Robbie said, reluctantly giving in to Mabel's demand, they sat on a stone bench facing the ocean under the June sun, the heat was getting stifling, have a drink from your cardboard cup, Mabel said to her thirsty parrot, drink, my Jerry, these two boys are young, one day they'll get it, go on and drink, they can't fathom how hard it is to be disabled, when your legs aren't what they used to be, tomorrow God will teach them what they don't understand today, eh Jerry, but as he sat down Petites Cendres, more supportive than she thought, put his hand on Mabel's knee, Petites Cendres was thinking of their art, the twilight art, art of the night, that those hooligans had disparaged with their stupid gibes, more racist and sexist than the usual taunts of a minority of men typically looked down upon as a kind of unknown species, didn't Yinn sew his own costumes, his mother helped, she was as much an artist as her son, but he designed them, every outfit a work of art, like a painting or a sculpture he applied himself to meticulously, carefully, until his eyes were lined with exhaustion, Petites Cendres knew Yinn's face so well, his skin, his eyelids, his eyes that seemed to well up, and turning to Robbie Petites Cendres said, you're right, Robbie, discrimination is a cancer, it consumes everything, oh I see a boat, a big freighter out there, Mabel said, it's big and if it makes too many waves the tiny boats will capsize, no, they won't be able to stay afloat and at sunrise tomorrow we'll find them strewn along the shore, I have to have a sip of water, she said, they'd been gone since early morning and Mabel wasn't used to walking in the sun for so long, she usually showed her birds and laid out her wares on the pier in the evening, at sunset or an hour later, she was thirsty, she said, offering her bottle of water to Robbie and Petites Cendres, but they weren't thirsty, I am, Mabel said insistently, I am thirsty, and the bag was weighing on her she said, looking out at the sea, the water roiling as the boat approached, the ship's lights were glittering even though it was day, the freighter was far away but waves were breaking in every direction, Mabel thought the small boats wouldn't make it, and Mick looked at his mother, such an elegant liar, he thought, impressing his friends at a literary cocktail party, she seemed so charming, even devoted, thought Mick, standing there with her husband, and Mick had joined them, neglecting the care of the teenage New York runaways in his care, rejected by their parents, kicked out of their homes, he'd taken them into his shelters, only because his sister Tammy was dying in a private clinic for anorexics, Tammy whom he loved so much and whom their parents hardly visited, though it was true that she refused to see them, could barely recognize them, she was lethargic, in a daze, not much more than a shadow, a hungry shadow, fed artificially if the shadow would keep still, sleep until evening, and bringing his face alongside hers, the face of his beloved sister, Mick had asked, you remember me, you remember me don't you, I'm Mick, it was us against them, they never loved us but you wouldn't run away with me and they're killing you, they let you be locked up in a cage, underfed despite all the care you're getting, they tell their friends you cost them a lot of money in this glass cage with plenty of nurses around, but despite the elaborate appearance of care, of saving you, they're letting you die, Mick told his sister at the clinic, you're leaving, you don't want to be with us anymore, I can hardly hear you breathe, Tammy, Tammy, Mick repeated as he took his sister's hand in his own at the fancy clinic where her too-brief existence would end, and now here he was, his parents had invited him to a cocktail party in their house by the sea, the house they had kicked him out of a few months earlier, with a bit of money, of course, should he want to continue his studies elsewhere, and then they'd summoned him back, Tammy wants to see you, they said, it was a request, possibly her last, they couldn't refuse Tammy, regardless of what Tammy and Mick thought their parents believed themselves to be considerate parents, they were good parents, they said, and Mick looked at this woman, his mother, so at ease among her fellow writers, the people she called her only true friends, Mick's parents were a good-looking couple in this world in which they saw only writers like themselves, a few painters too, they were fulfilled by each other, a union Mick's mother had described in her books as prolific, fecund, they had written many books, the two of them, their marriage had been simply perfect, a couple without children, but they'd committed themselves to a family construct without really anticipating what they were getting into, they'd been young, too bohemian perhaps, inexperienced, yes, Mick observed his mother, they looked like each other, her femininity etched in his bonier features, he was like a disfigured portrait of his mother and no doubt despite her minimal affection for her children she recognized herself in him, but derisively and without satisfaction, Mick thought, she didn't like her son's touch or for him to be near though she did feel pity for Tammy, Tammy was no more than a child to be pitied, she would have preferred that the poor child, wayward and wretched, were not hers, that she might have escaped the shame, as ashamed of Tammy as she was of Mick, the androgynous son or whatever they were calling them today, she preferred to ignore him, to abandon him, for him to stay away from her and from his father, from his parents and their happy union, for him not to spoil everything, before the two of them our lives had been serene, calm, and then everything came undone, Tammy an alcoholic almost since childhood, and the other one, the boy, he wasn't even a boy, at Trinity College they were about to nail him to a tree, his classmates hated him and later almost threw him off the school roof and it fell back on us, the parents, two deviant children, why should we have loved them, respected them, tell me that, Mick caught his mother's eye below her straw hat, that's what she thinks of us, but in that moment Mick's mother was remarking that perhaps there'd been some progress in her son's attitude, she appreciated that at least he hadn't come dressed like Michael Jackson with bright red lips or something, no, he was wearing black shorts, a black shirt, and his hair was shorter, he was sparing his parents, it was because of his sister too, who only had a few days to live, he was thinking of his sister not his parents, Mick's mother thought, he never gave them any consideration, how hard it had been to raise difficult children, difficult, unacceptable children, if only they'd known, oh, if they had known, someone asked Mick's mother what her son was doing in New York, if he was studying and what college he was attending, she answered haughtily, no, he's working, for one social cause or another, I don't know, he's an odd duck, it's always a mystery what he's up to, but Mick jumped in and added that with the help of some Catholic priests and Black pastors they'd opened shelters, yes, for children in the ghetto, Mick's father said isn't it hard, what a hard thing to do but so worthwhile, it was almost as if he approved of his eccentric son, but the father's voice sounded detached, like he was discussing some historical fact from one of the books he'd written on the inevitable unfolding of history, the father's tone struck Mick as professorial, his daughter dying alone in a clinic and her parents enjoying themselves all the while at a cocktail party on their terrace by the sea, and Mick's mother confided to a writer friend that they'd bought a semi-detached with a blue swimming pool and a whole bloom of silver palms so it would be so quiet and peaceful when they were writing their books, yes, they were successful writers, Mick thought, with the money they'd made over the years they could have saved Tammy, she was like a child drowning, screaming, without anyone being able to hear her from the shore they watched her die, Mick thought, but his father seemed cordial now for some reason, he leaned in to Mick and said in his ear we can talk to each other like men, can't we, come home, we miss you, let's not lose faith for Tammy, we learned yesterday that she could get better, you know, she's getting the best care, but everything would be better if you were with us, it's hard for your mother, look, I know she told you not to come back, but you know her, she's always so intense when she's writing, I'd like it if you could forgive her and come back to live with us, are you listening to me Mick, and hearing the sudden sincerity in his father's voice he wondered if he was being genuine or if he was trying to cast some sort of spell on his son, and Mick thought of Tammy beneath the white sheet at the clinic, he could hear her calling, deliriously, reaching for life, she was mumbling a few names familiar to him, the names of friends, and out of nowhere she uttered Mai's, she was remembering her friend Mai, babbling incomprehensibly, they were roller skating, Tammy and Mai, Mai always out front and Tammy doing her best to follow but that night the fog rolling in off the ocean was thick and they were lost, Mai, Tammy called out imploringly, where's Mai, will she come see me, the fog is so thick, I can't breathe, you have to agree to eat, Mick said as he placed Tammy's hand on the white sheet, her frail hand streaked with blue, Mai, Tammy, what a party, she murmured, that's how it began, yes, with parties at night in the field, at Manuel's, yes, and then Tammy sank back into silence and seemed not to remember anything, don't worry so much about your sister, she'll be all right, Mick's father said, but what an ordeal for your mother, remember this is still your house, this is your home, this is where you grew up, we have to talk man to man, you understand, Mick, why don't you listen, you're so stubborn, Mick wanted to leave, to leave his father and his mother forever and he couldn't figure out what mad hope kept him, was there a chance for Tammy, could there be, and Daniel thought about the *Southern Light* sailing out on the water, Mélanie and Mai might have weighed anchor by Fortress Island where they would see the sea turtles from the sanctuary, shouldn't we believe, like Nelson Mandela, that the most powerful weapon of change in the world is education and, first and foremost, education for the youngest, it was with this philosophy in mind that Daniel's father and his biologist friends had created an aquarium for endangered sea turtles out at the bird sanctuary, veterinarians were working there around the clock, operating on these animals that were victims of human abuse, of our negligence, they'd flip the animals over onto their shells to work on them, their short legs or beaks bound up in plastic or cloaked in black oil from the ships, and schoolchildren came to watch the births and rebirths, all over the world people watched videos of the rescues, in Spanish, English, German, and Daniel was thrilled, his daughter too, that the program was such a success though at the same time he knew how precarious animal and ecological projects were, what had been built up could be destroyed in an instant by the massive ignorance of those who just used nature, who wore it down, but wasn't it more important than anything to believe in Mandela's words, in his call for respect from the far side of an ocean littered with human debris, a poet's words hovering over the void, Mai had written to her father that she had seen one of the sea turtles swimming in the aquarium, holding its beak near some lettuce and finally, calm and healed, she was able to walk through the aquarium, to feed the animals without the aid of veterinarians, what a joy, Papa, Mai had written to her father, she sent a photograph, a picture she had taken of the young veterinarians who were also involved in the rescues, the sea turtles in the oceans and along the Coral Coast were precarious, threatened, I've never seen anything so upsetting, Papa, visitors to the island entertaining themselves on the sea turtles' backs, on their shells, smashing them with their weight, it's horrible, Papa, these cruel, reprehensible acts, and reading Mai's text on his phone Daniel could almost hear her crying, but Mélanie and Mai had probably set sail, back in the boat and especially if the wind was light, in June the weather could turn quickly, torrential rain whirlpooling on the water and throwing sailboats off course, and thinking of Mai Daniel was seized by the thought of the secrets Mai kept from her father and never revealed, though he thought Mai was the kindest of his children, always solicitous when he was sad or discouraged as writers at work frequently are, she would show up, hug him, reassure him, but he knew nothing about Mai, despite her childlike candour she was always so secretive, she confided more in her mother Mélanie though Daniel had no sense of that either, the mother–daughter relationship was another mystery separating him from Mai, Mai and Mélanie seemed to be one person undivided by any clear autonomy, or two people equally determined and fierce in the defence of their quiet complicity, and wasn't it the same with Augustino, what did a father really know about his children, thought Daniel, the *Southern Light* had set sail, catching an easterly wind, and Mélanie, the captain on board, felt the softness of the wind in her dancing hair, Mai cried when she saw the sea turtles, tears of joy as much as sadness, the torture inflicted on the animals always broke her heart, they suffer because of us, and perhaps there was another reason for the grief in her bright eyes, one that Mélanie was trying to understand, leaning into the noisy waves that rocked the boat as the words tumbled out, words Mélanie could barely hear, for a second Mélanie had held Mai by the waist saying, tell me, yes, tell me, but the *Southern Light* churned with the waves and Mélanie didn't hear the monologue of uncontrollable grief bursting out beside her, Mai blamed herself for neglecting her friend Tammy, she had visited her at the clinic but was afraid, her friend was a ghost of her former self, Mai couldn't bear the sight of Tammy so frail, so humiliated, and Mélanie, attentive now, stopped the engine and said you need to see Tammy, you have to go back to the clinic and give her courage, the courage to say no, but Mama, she can't hear anything anymore, she's in a strange coma, she's slipping away, she doesn't want to stay anymore, I don't want to see her go down like that, I don't want to see her go, her parents always treated her so unfairly, didn't you always tell me, Mama, that we are responsible for each other, I am responsible, I know it, we all are, did I say that, Mélanie asked Mai, isn't that somewhat intransigent, I never said that, Mélanie said, and Mai heard the engine shudder, the boat shaken by the waves, the tears dried quickly on her cheeks and four white herons that had been nesting in the mangroves appeared, lifting off the water, their flight so filled with purpose, the herons' long slender necks lined up against the blue sky speckled with a few clouds, no, I couldn't have said that, Mélanie repeated, we each have our own destiny, whether it's bad or benign, look Mama they're flying over us, Mai shouted and quickly she took out her

camera, kissing her mother distractedly, and Mélanie wondered where her daughter's face was behind those piercings,
her ears, eyebrows, piercings everywhere shimmering in
the golden light of the sun on Mai's face, the child she hardly
ever saw, she'd felt guilty about it since Mai had moved out,
and her sons, she saw them so seldom too, even when the
children were young, with her activism, her social and politi-
cal commitments she'd been too busy and now her children
were busy in turn, she'd been too absorbed by her wounded
but never-diminished love for Augustino, for whose return
she would wait forever when there might be no return at
all, and in the hum of the waves Mélanie thought she could
hear her mother's voice saying, as she used to, oh, my dear
daughter, can a woman bring up the children she adores
and hold a position of leadership too, tell me, we women
often have the feeling that we're taking advantage of our
liberty, that we're not entitled to it, especially when our
children are born, you will see with each step you take, my
dear Mélanie, that we're alone, quite alone, but I know that
you'll keep moving forward, above all you must feel no
doubt, and it was Mère's voice making itself felt in Mélanie's
heart, Mélanie missed her mother Esther every minute, her
absence gnawing at Mélanie's happiness in life, and standing near the mast in her white shorts Mai marvelled at the
flight of the herons, we should head back before the glint
of noon, the midday light so blinding at sea, they ought to
head back, Mélanie thought, but the wind, the air, the heat,
it made her lazy and languid, laziness was so contrary to
her principles, she straightened up, stretching out her arms
as if she meant to dive into the waves, it was such a pictur-
esque June morning, too bad Mai felt such boundless grief
for her friend Tammy, and Mélanie thought it's not true, she

might have said that to Mai once, but no, it couldn't be true,
it's not even possible for us to be responsible for each other,
no, that couldn't be true, even if she had said so and repeated
as much to her children, now she wondered how she'd
been able to utter such an idea, where did it come from, it
was hard enough to be responsible for yourself, wasn't that
what she'd told her children, during the refugee crisis perhaps, when she and Mère had agreed to welcome them into
their home, Julio, Jenny, Marie-Sylvie de la Toussaint and
their families, wasn't that a basic human response to so
much tragedy, they owned several houses on the island and
they let them stay in Mère's house, which she had gener-
ously lent, choosing instead to live with her daughter and
her family, surely when she had acted on such a charitable
impulse she had told the children we are responsible, yes,
you are responsible too, you have everything, you are children of privilege, the words had marked Augustino forever,
he felt responsible for everyone, each and every person,
had the words been too much for him, Mélanie wondered,
and Petites Cendres on Atlantic Boulevard looked out at the
sea that was no longer so calm, replaying in his head those
late nights at the cabaret, the stage and the bar around it
bathed in red light, it was the end of the night, almost day-
break, a slight grime settling over the city, in the streets, and
on the sidewalks, where the bruisers hung out, gesticulating
and shouting with bottles of beer between their legs, and
on the second floor of the Saloon, Petites Cendres remembered that on the ground floor was an underground porn
theatre, the cinema would be open, a few customers dozing,
on the second floor Yinn and Victoire waiting for each other,
the only ones at the bar, Jason in his lighting booth wasn't
ready for Yinn yet, fiddling with his lights and the colours

for the next day, he was standing apart, on the other side of the bar and the stage, and Petites Cendres rediscovered that disillusioned side of Yinn, how deflated he was after a performance, still in costume, the black dress with the white collar and the Afro wig with its thousand knots and curls, and Victoire was in a woman's outfit that was hers now, she was dignified but so excessively modest it made her clumsy, and Petites Cendres, moved by Yinn's expression, the pallor of Yinn's hollow cheeks under the bulging forehead, the look of utter weariness he wore as he smoked his cigarettes and drank his cherry cocktails, Petites Cendres could hear Yinn and Victoire talking quietly, Victoire was telling Yinn that she had won back her job as an engineer, a woman engineer, she said, it's an experiment and I have no idea how hard it's gonna be, Victoire said, but you, Yinn, you're so inspiring, you bring your friends into the struggle, the fight I'll never stop fighting because it's mine, yours, ours, you know the military accepts transgender troops now, we have to believe in this invisible revolution, like you always say, Yinn, we're living it from the inside, I think that's how you describe it, from the inside, it's invisible on a moral level, sure, but everything will become more and more concrete and more visible with the new laws, everyone will have their place, Yinn said, which is as it should be, and Victoire's voice, high and a bit shrill, got sadder, became more masculine, but wars, she said, wars don't change, they never will, I get letters from soldiers' mothers, they've lost a son in Vietnam, or sons, always near the end of a battle in which four hundred soldiers have died, you have to beat through the bush to find them, blood spurting from bodies hidden by grass and mud, if they're still standing they're holding each other up with one arm, one hand, survivors, short men with bruised faces under their steel helmets, at the base a nurse approaches them, their broken limbs, they say save my brother, this is my brother, save him, and then they can no longer stand and they fall, and Victoire's breath quickened, wars are all the same, she repeated, the same, what can I say to the parents of those dead sons, I've killed too, I've seen their desperate faces under the black helmets and thought the same thing, he could be my brother, my friend, and a profound silence settled over the two friends, let's forget that tonight, Victoire, Yinn said as Jason brought his ladder down from the lighting booth, the night was ending for everyone, several of the queens had left and he would go change now, the most upsetting thing, Victoire said in the same disconsolate voice, was when one of them asked a nurse or a doctor if he was going to be all right and they said yes, of course, the soldier didn't even know about the two bleeding wounds cut into his belly, you could see his guts through the two gaping, bleeding wounds in his stomach, yes, the ambulance is here, the nurse would say, young man, I think you will be fine, sleep now, don't worry, everything will be okay, they were only children and the fighting in the rice paddies had been going on for ten days, no one spoke of courage, the fighting started early in the morning and the bodies piled up throughout the afternoon, wars are the same, Victoire said again, and although Yinn seemed weary of listening Victoire went on, sharing the nightmare stories, this veteran who wrote to me, Victoire said, he'd killed a North Vietnamese with his bayonet while at his side a friend finished off another enemy soldier with a .45, a double murder, a double crime, two companions killing side by side as if it were old hat, a gesture that trivi-alizes the horrors of war, killing is meaningless, living or

dying is meaningless, the veteran is now a businessman, a
father, a respectable husband on the surface but he's haunted
by what he did, by that double murder he committed, with
a partner, he wrote to me that he thinks of committing suicide, what happened haunts him too much, he can't live
normally anymore, but no one knows his secret, not his
wife or his children, he lies in bed at night and can't unsee
the tearful face grimacing in pain, a pain so awful the soldier
can't even describe it, no, the veteran said, I cannot live
with this memory, I see his face over and over, the face of
the enemy in front of me and the frail figure buckling, this
man I split in two when I pulled the trigger, and then Victoire
fell silent and Yinn repeated, I told you, Victoire, you really
should forget, you must try to forget, and as Brilliant walked
Misha along Atlantic Boulevard, he had Misha on a leash,
he was jogging and the dog was running alongside him, for
the longest time Misha had refused to leave Angel's room,
Brilliant called and called and Misha stayed flat on the
ground, he had stopped moving, it's time to go out, Brilliant
said to Misha, time to obey your master, Misha's big paws
finally pushing him up and now, even though Misha was
sad, he was following Brilliant, but his head was bent low
and he trotted alongside without his usual pleasure, usually
he loved going out with Brilliant but now the sky seemed
oppressive, the sun was hot on his fur and he was thirsty,
though he knew Brilliant would give him a drink in his
bowl soon because Brilliant thought of everything, he'd
been a comfort to Misha even when Misha was at his unhap-
piest, even during the hurricane, and during hurricanes
before, he'd almost been swept away by the storm, swimming for hours between two rotten boards from a destroyed
house, before he and hundreds of pets in danger like him

were rescued, no, he'd never been as unhappy as he was now, but Brilliant said to Misha, listen, that's enough, think of our friend Angel walking by our side, or flying rather, how wonderful it must be for Angel to be able to fly like that, he's an astronaut, he needs to visit other planets on his space flight, you believe that don't you, Misha, it's time for you to think of your own destiny and to find your wonderful dog smile, everyone loves to see your wolf smile, you with your fangs bared, yeah, it's nice to trust you but you're still a wolf, Misha, there are lots of cyclists out this morning along Atlantic Boulevard, some of them talking on their phones with one hand on the handlebars, future accident victims of mine, as a nurse's assistant I'm the one who patches them up when they come in to the emergency banged up and in shock after being hit by a car, they're reckless modern dreamers on their bicycles, dreamers chatting recklessly on their phones, whether they're sitting in a car or on their bikes you can hear them babbling away, hey, Brilliant, a cyclist hailed Brilliant with one hand, holding his phone up to one ear with the other, hey, Brilliant, we don't see much of you anymore, we don't see you writing on the walls at fishermen's taverns, are you writing your book, your oral opus as you used to say, where are you, and where are you going with your dog, he looks pretty sad, I'm off to Pelican Beach, Brilliant said, we're just hot, that's all, but as soon as we get there we'll have some fun, eh Misha, we'll run in the waves, Misha, it's pretty far, several miles from here, Pelican Beach is past the airport, it's a forgotten beach, nobody goes there anymore, the cyclist said, excuse me, Brilliant, my phone's ringing, it's my girlfriend, we have a date tonight, hello, hi sexy, the cyclist babbled away on his phone, hi, are you waiting for me to have lunch on the beach, I'm almost there, I'll be right there, kisses, yeah, lots of kisses, the cyclist pressed his lips against the screen, here, kisses, he made some more kissing sounds and hung up, what were you telling me, Brilliant, that you're now a nurse's assistant, that job would totally disgust me, wow, careful, that truck brushed right by me, bye Brilliant, my girlfriend's waiting, man, those trucks, they're such lousy drivers, so you're still writing on walls, Brilliant, what a weirdo you are, yeah, exactly, Brilliant answered, but the man was gone, away on his bicycle barely touching the ground, swallowed up by the horizon, Angel had loved the forgotten beach because hardly anyone ever went there, and I said to Angel's mother, Lena, don't worry, I'm taking Misha for a walk, I'm going to take him with me to Pelican Beach for the ceremony, come join us later with Lucia, you can come in Lucia's car because now Lucia has the car I gave her, there you go, and I'm going to tell everyone the good news, no one will ever guess, it's going to be such a surprise, they won't believe it, because one day we cry and the next we're laughing and enjoying ourselves, listen to me, Misha, life is full of adventures, some things are complete surprises, you can't see everything coming, Atlantic Boulevard is all grandiose palaces and big pink hotels, there are no alleys or bars under the acacias, and along the way there are only merchants selling lemonade and every colour of ice cream in the trucks set up by the ocean, yes, but I've got some vodka with me, you'll have some refreshing cold water and me, well, I'll have a vodka lemonade of course, we could also stop at one of the pink hotels and I'd order a screwdriver and you could go drink from a fountain like you do at the Acacia Gardens, we could do that, yeah, but they're waiting for us and it's Angel's soul giving the orders today, I'm pretty sure they'll serve us champagne at noon, Misha, don't be so slow, run a little, hey, what will Angel say, with his piercing eyes, his eagle eyes, he sees everything now, he's an astronaut, he sees everything from up there, what would he think of you, so beaten down, you're walking so slowly, come on, do what I do, smell the jasmine, it's such a gorgeous day, how can you be so depressed, just think how euphoric you'll be when I take off your leash and you can finally run in the waves, in the ocean, and you'll see how I surprise them with my news, you'll see, Misha, I'll be jumping for joy when I'm able to tell them, Misha, and Misha's ears perked up as Brilliant walked ahead of him with his nervous, bouncing gait, Misha deciding to follow, slowly, and on that heavenly June morning, standing in his garden with the chicks chirping and their mother cackling, Daniel was thrilled to get a letter from Eddy, written on stationery like Jean-Mathieu used for his letters to Charles, the large masculine handwriting was a testament to the young waiter's vigour, Eddy, hungry for the pleasures of life, and reading the letter Daniel forgot for a moment the suffering he felt as he worked on his book, Eddy materializing in his garden through the mystical presence of the written word, we've lost the habit of reading a letter when it's not on a screen, Eddy's words, the inky scribbles of a pen on paper, they had a symbolic, almost spiritual value, thought Daniel, Eddy's presence bringing back not only the memory of the waiter in the white jacket and black tie who'd first welcomed him at a country hotel in Scotland at the literary festival but also the whole landscape of that place, the long climb into the forest that last night for the writers' banquet and every word spoken during the speeches that evening, and Daniel wondered if the words had been heard or even listened to, the absence of certain writers at the festival was like a death knell, no one knew why exactly they'd been prevented from attending the festival, whether they were being tortured or were captive somewhere, thought Daniel, writers from Iran, Africa, Vietnam, and Eddy wrote to Daniel, as I promised, dear Daniel, I carefully noted when each writer arrived and left, and those who came back to meet at the hotel after the event, that young writer, Henri, he came back to see us, he was alone this time, not with the girls, the secretaries and agents that had surrounded him, no, he was alone, he said his books were selling better but that wasn't his first priority, he told me he wanted to take time to reflect so that given his character, of which you're aware, Daniel, knowing his romantic tendency to depression, I kept sharp objects away from him and asked that the velvet cords on the curtains in his room be hidden away, because with him who can say, he told me he walks in the forest and goes to the mountain, the mountain where your festival was held, and he is still in that dreary mood that worried you so, dear Daniel, did you recognize something of your tormented son in him, I believe the beauty of our lakes and forests will do Henri good and that his face will take on a healthier glow, that by visiting our wonderful country his health will improve and he'll regain his good humour, won't he, Daniel, you understand when I say that it's difficult for me to feel too much sympathy for someone so morose, but he's your friend and I wanted to tell you that he's still with us and busy writing, perhaps he is not in the best health physically, I dare say sports strengthen the body but also the mind, and as you can see I am still apprenticing in the same hotel in Scotland, but, curious nomad that I am, I'll be leaving soon for a second apprenticeship as a waiter in New Zealand, I can't wait to learn about that magnificent country and, through my humble waiter's profession to make my way across the earth and discover its magnificence, to meet many girls at the same time, love strengthens the heart and also the mind, and I wanted to tell you, dear Daniel, that I saw the London poet's red-headed daughters, the poet is deceased, alas, the minstrel whose poetry charmed us so and whom I remember, his joyful company when we shared a few drinks at the festival, every year he was there at the hotel and treated me as if I was his friend, Eddy, he said to me, you're my friend, you may recite my verse, I drink to your adventurous youth, my friend, and may love never disappoint you as it has disappointed my old heart, there is no recovery from that, but sir, I said to him, you have the loveliest daughters in the world, and when I saw the red-headed daughters of my dedicated poet friend from London I was so pleased, we talked about him, the disappeared poet, and likewise we shared fond memories of you on that occasion at the Celtic Tavern, during your stay in Scotland, when I was your waiter, dear Daniel, you may remember that group of young girls having lunch in the park, they were five and one of them was about to get married, they were laughing, carefree, one of them bought your book and asked me at length to explain it, right, as if a book can be explained, she wanted to know if your work is autobiographical, it seems that way, although not being a writer I cannot judge, she wanted to know if the young man you describe in your book, the one with mysterious designs, the alienated one, if that young man is by chance your son, you seem to know him so well, oh, my frivolous young friends asking writers embarrassing questions as usual, I've noticed that my poet friends always answer with irritation, the girls wanted to know whether you write at night or during the day and about your most secret habits, but I can be glad that my friends, that group of young women you saw in the park, all of them, though seemingly so flighty, have read your book, they read it to the end they told me, which is what I wanted to write to you, dear Daniel, because of the friendship I felt for you, and dear Daniel, I will end my letter here to go back to the bar where my customers await, some of them are regulars, though none inspire such happiness as the London poet, the minstrel, and his red-headed daughters, or even you, Daniel, who amused and entertained me with your words and with your hope for the future, which I share, and Daniel finished reading Eddy's note and heard the sound of wheels, a rustle of steel in the leaves behind the hedge of young palms in the garden over the chirping of the birds, J'aime appeared in his wheelchair, Daniel recognized his eyes sparkling in the morning light, J'aime's head and the dangling arms that made him seem so vulnerable in the chair, as if his arms were casting about for some stability they couldn't find, the unpredictable chaos of his nerves forced them to move continuously, but J'aime's gaze was poised, he stared straight ahead, unflinching in his serenity, my friend, said J'aime, spontaneous as always, I wanted to bring you an invitation to my show, an exhibition of my paintings is going up at the movie theatre where I give my weekly lectures, you remember, on films, some more recent and some old films, you didn't know I was a painter, maybe down the road I'll be a writer, but for a long time I've been a painter like my father is, my father passed on his passion for colour, I want to stimulate the imagination of artists who suffer from the same disability, and art is the path to joy, isn't it, I paint what I see, and my vision isn't the same as other people's, from my low angle I see a universe that is sort of elongated, but I see the sky and the trees like everyone else, and I want to paint the air, it's so hot this time of year, it feels like a fruit bursting, a mango, right, a mango, they're in season, and Daniel listened to the irrepressible J'aime, whose words, despite the furrows carved into them by the fervour of his breathing, the syncopation of his effort to pronounce each one, his words were radiant, like that June morning, Mélanie and Mai floating aboard the *Southern Light* at that very hour, of course I'll come to your exhibit, Daniel said, I'll see you there, J'aime exclaimed as he wheeled himself away to the street, Daniel could no longer see him but he could hear his chair, J'aime, like Eddy, a transcendent messenger on a day which in the morning had seemed frightening and heavy, he had awoken from his sleep inside the nightmare of the Young Man, a murderer whose witness he had become by telling his story, and in a shady corner between the pink walls of the big hotels, under a tent protecting them from the sun, Brilliant spotted a mother and her children singing on Atlantic Boulevard, Brilliant, and Misha behind him, head down, Misha ambled toward them, the young mother was playing an out-of-tune keyboard, her children standing beside her, a Black family, they were stunning, Brilliant thought when he saw them, what a joy it was to hear them singing so early in the morning, Brilliant lived at night and as far as he was concerned mornings shouldn't even exist, with their dull pallor and so full of tasks, but Brilliant had to get up very early in the morning now, the emergencies at the hospital didn't wait for daylight, this is Angie, she's ten years old, the young mother said as one of her children, holding her skateboard

under her arm, was about to sing, this is Angelina, she's
seven, she said flatly, and this is my oldest daughter, Annette,
she's sixteen, in the burning air their music sounded dis-
jointed, like the sound of the piano, but the sound of their
young voices singing in unison filled the air with a wistful
indolence and Brilliant said to Misha, didn't I tell you, Misha,
we must sing, he who cried yesterday sings today, didn't I
say that Misha, and all night, through the muddy waters of
his dreams, the Young Man heard the judge's sentence, the
judge was of that race of people the Young Man despised,
your lawyer and your psychologist are trying in vain to make
your case, but you cannot escape it, we are delaying your
trial in order to collect the evidence against you, the judge
shouted, it shall be the death penalty for you, even if the
victims' families ask for forgiveness we will not listen, God
is our only judge and only He can deliver justice, they tell
me, these families who want clemency, because they are
Christians they want mercy for you, you killed their mothers, fathers, and children, they're praying for you, but do
you hear what I am saying to you, Young Man, it'll be the
death penalty, we were discussing it as you paced in your
cell, biting your nails, soon you will be led along the wall,
along the cells of the condemned, and so shall your life
end, the Young Man heard this sentence during the night,
for nights on end he heard the judge and his sentence, the
Young Man saw a courtroom with faces and forms he
couldn't make out, the place of judgement was a cave from
which he was unable to escape, only the judge seemed to
be there, the Young Man would say I am cold, I am hungry,
it's too damp for me here but only a hostile muttering
answered his complaint, you will never be cold enough,
you will never be hungry enough, die, and die quickly, but

the baleful murmurs fell silent, and Pastor Anna, yes, it was her, her head covered in blood, Pastor Anna extended her hand to the Young Man and said, come, my child, we're going back to your parents' house, where is your home, do you remember, though following Pastor Anna the Young Man couldn't find the street or his parents' house, maybe they had moved, or else they'd renounced him, they hadn't visited him for weeks, yes, that could be it, the Young Man remembered those sleepless nights but he showered, he scrubbed himself clean as if to chase away the frightening images, and when the guard had brought him back to his cell he could hear only the laughter and sadistic jeers of the other prisoners, as if the prison were his courtroom, as if they were the ones who would judge him tomorrow, their scathing words condemned him, men who'd committed a lifetime of crimes, they were thieves, killers, and plunderers, and they mocked him for losing his murderer's virginity, what was he to them, a pitiful novice who had almost succumbed to Pastor Anna's smile, at the last moment he had almost lost his desire to follow through with his crime because she'd smiled at him and said it's not too late, go home to your parents, it is never too late for God's mercy, the pastor had soiled him with her God and her religion, hadn't the Young Man felt himself recoiling at the last moment from the evil he'd set out to accomplish, for him the evil was good, a purification, Black blood had to be shed and shed again and again as he had written in his manifesto of hate, and as he paced back and forth in his cell the Young Man knew that his parents had reneged on their past, a past that clamoured with the voices of hatred, they had brought up the Young Man to forget the past, there had never been racism in their city, they said, never in their country, never anything so dishonourable, his parents were respectable citizens who silenced the voices of hatred by denying them, who repeated incessantly that the past was the past, all races must live together in harmony they said, that was how the Young Man had been brought up, that silence, that stifling of ancient voices, had been a good education yet he, the Young Man, remembered all the same that he had been born long after, that he'd been born during his parents' reign of silence, what his parents described as a resurrection of justice for people of colour at last, and ignoring their conniving, ignoring his parents' cunning, their hypocritical revolution, the Young Man had opened a book of his own making, filled with pictures of a not-so-distant past in which he discovered his true masters, dead now, they had died powerless, almost, slain because they had refused racial assimilation, they were heroes, the Young Man thought, they were his people, heroes had blood on their hands Martin Luther King said, and the governor, what a hero he'd been for the Young Man, they said he was racist like it was a disease that would gradually poison him, which is what happened, he would die of it, and now the governor and his hatred triumphed in the heart of the Young Man, hadn't two hundred and sixty-six thousand whites voted for him, like him they thought down with Blacks, keep them out of our universities, our schools, we don't want them, over the billowing voices of hatred the governor had shouted, I raised the salaries of the Black teachers and they complained, I always said segregation was a good thing, for centuries, for generations we whites and people of colour lived in peace and fairness, why should that stop, everyone has his own religion, his own church, and that's the way it was, a few dissenting voices among you and that balance is undone, the rebellion of the few has disrupted our communities, segregation will now be mandatory at the University of Alabama, the governor had courted extremist voters and what the Young Man admired most was that under the governor churches burned, the Birmingham Baptist Church was bombed, though only four young Black girls were assassinated, no more, the Young Man would do better, in memory of the acclaimed governor he revered, the Young Man would do so much better at the New Hope Methodist Church where sometimes he went to pray, or at least pretended to, though in fact he wanted to study the place and those who went there for their Sunday prayers, and as he was reflecting the Young Man saw a face between the bars of his cell, a man of imposing stature, and the man said to the Young Man, I am your chaplain, your pastor, you may need me, the man spoke without anger, almost softly, I recognize you, the Young Man said nothing, his mouth was frozen, numb, the Young Man thought, so you're the one responsible for everything, you and the others before you, but he also felt that he was speaking these words to the man in front of him, on the other side of the bars, in the moment he must have looked so pathetic in his numbered prison jumpsuit, he wished his words could strike the man, blows to his face, but the man, the chaplain or pastor, seemed at ease, yes, the Young Man thought, it's you, you were a Black singer in a church in Atlanta, the preacher's son, your mother played the organ, the Young Man said, I recognize you, despite his tendency to go quiet, fearful as soon as anyone approached, you remember, don't you, you were barely ten years old and your friends refused to play with you because they were white and their mother wouldn't let them, you remember, I'm sure you do, how could you possibly have dreamed of changing the world, how could you have been so brazen, it's outrageous, and yet my parents listened to you and followed you, they were among the hundred thousand people walking with you during that famous march, they were there, you were a preacher from the South, a Black boy who sang in church and who liked to deliver long sermons, the son of a preacher, a hundred years had passed since slavery was abolished and yet you went on about it as some terrible thing that was going on today and white people in the streets begged you to shut up, they said they would lynch you and your people and the whites walking with you, you were going to reform the politics of hatred, right, and you could have done it too, that was it, and then his words evaporated in sullen plumes as the imposing man spoke, don't hesitate to call on me if I can help you, the man said, to me all the men here are brothers, children of God, don't bait me with your religion, the Young Man said, angry, and don't visit me anymore, I don't want to hear any more from you, you disgust me, the Young Man said, you're disgusted with yourself, the man on the other side of the bars said, the man who was free while the Young Man was not, one day you may be in need, don't hesitate to ask me to come, I'll leave you now, I have to lead a prayer group for repentant inmates, there's less pain in repentance, the man said as he walked toward the iron staircase, from his cage the Young Man shouted an insult that the man didn't seem to hear but inside he was trembling, so it's true, they want the death penalty, the Young Man thought, but they won't succeed, the death penalty is what everyone wants, there's a sickening debate about the death penalty that will help me, yes, I'll have the activists on my side and I will mock them, Christians who have no conception of the majesty of killing, even my victims' parents, their brothers and sisters whose existence I snuffed out with my .45, bang, they're crying out for me to be absolved, we must forgive him they say, but the Young Man remembered the face of one person who refused to let it go, the picture of a young man in a newspaper or on television who held his inconsolable mother in his arms, his face with his lips tight, he'd lost his sister in the massacre, his mother had lost her daughter, and the expression on the sculptural face of the young man was one of revenge as he held his anguished mother in her distress, her silent distress, suppressed by her Christian resignation, his vengeful, livid expression, an anger without succour because nothing would quell the young man's anger as religion calmed his mother's grief, the young man's eyes said you, you murderer, I'll strangle you with my own two hands, the state is slow to lay you down on your deathbed because, so they say, there's a shortage of the poison they'll use to kill you being made in the labs, and all over the world, in every country, people are hesitating and it's delaying your execution, they're dithering and it's keeping the poison, the venom, from being injected into your veins but I know how to find you and I will come, for my sister, for my mother, for those you have annihilated with your games, because it was just a game for you, this slaughter, a hunt inside a church from which your victims were unable to flee, come evening they would have gathered for a family meal, one person and the next around a table sharing red rice and corn, and what did you do, never again will they be together around a table, never again, my mother doesn't smile anymore, she can no longer raise her head to the sky, you killed her in her soul and I'm going to come for you, you white bastard, I'm going to hang you, yes, that boy's expression obsessed the Young Man because it held a hatred that mirrored his own for the Black race, maybe the Young Man would have to fight him, to fight the constant reminder that he had an equal among the enemy race, they were the same age and had the same build, and then the Young Man thought about what he'd written in his manifesto of hate, that all the way back to the 1936 Olympics, even in the Nazi era, Black athletes had outpaced whites, such arrogance needed to be punished, men and women about to become the most odious collaborators in the extermination of an entire people were applauding the Black athletes on their podiums, we saw the runner Jesse Owens accepting his gold medal in Berlin, the white race slavishly bowing before the Black race, wrote the Young Man in his manifesto of hate, was there anything more scandalous, more repugnant than that, everywhere Black athletes were winning, there would be no surrender, this needed to be their end, there was no other solution than the end of the Black and yellow and brown races, the Young Man had written in his manifesto, and then there would be peace, he thought, yes, he had already begun, no one knew who he was before the day of his crimes and now his name was everywhere, though what comfort was there in notoriety when he felt listless, apathetic, numb in the face of the verdict that was near, how could he rest, even if he was being terrorized in his cell, yes, him, the hero of the White Supremacist Youth, the cleansing had begun, a clean sweep, yes, in a church with his .45, bang bang and they fell and fell, it was easier than he'd expected the Young Man thought, and in the shadow of the big hotels with their pink façades Brilliant told Misha that he remembered seeing the Black family singing as he'd taken a stroll in the evening, singing to passersby and to tourists, and at the end of each song the mother said, always in a slightly weary tone, you just heard a song she wrote herself, Angelina was seven years old and Angie was ten, and Misha followed Brilliant with his head bowed and drank from the fountain but still felt an unquenchable summer thirst, Brilliant remembering that the singers' voices sounded even finer in the night air on a warm evening, and the notes on the piano even more unsettling, and between songs the mother taught the youngest to read or they would do their homework, even in summer, and from the terraces of the big hotels tourists watched disdainfully, and a small girl from one of those families might escape her nanny, the parents busy elsewhere and distracted by the posh poolside parties around the shimmering water gleaming green from the reflected palms, and the girl would come up to Angie, who was ten years old, and give her a few pennies and say with a foreign accent, you're ten years old like me, hi, Angie, that's your name, isn't it, Angie, I wish I could make music just like you, Angie's brown hand took the hand of the white girl, they seemed to be looking at each other almost lovingly until the nanny appeared, took the child, and whispered didn't your mother tell you never to talk to strangers, didn't your mother forbid this, naughty girl, I'm going to tell your mother, and when the rich girl was gone Angie started to sing, her melody tinged with tender melancholy while Annette's fingers pounded out clumsy sounds from the keys, and Brilliant strode along Atlantic Boulevard, breathing in the smell of those summer evenings when the birds continue to sing even as the sun sets and he happened to come across the young veteran Samson sitting on a bench facing the ocean with the dog he'd named Miracle because, as Samson explained, the dog he'd adopted at the Veterans and Dogs Coalition Shelter had healed him, every day he saved him from his nightmares, he'd survived an explosion in Afghanistan but suffered head trauma, my dog saves me when I have epileptic seizures, when I can't remember where I am, he's always there for me, I call him Miracle, he's my therapy against the flashbacks, the explosion keeps on whistling in my brain and it hurts, Samson was almost moaning, we're two wounded heroes, he and I, for a long time he was alone and mistreated, my poor dog, and look, Brilliant, how dignified he is now, and so protective, because I brought him back to life too, I brought him out of his shell, his misery, tell me, Brilliant, what did I name him, I've forgotten, the doctor said that the seizures and the effects of the injury will last another year, and sitting beside Samson, his eyes shielded behind dark glasses because since his return from Afghanistan he couldn't bear the light and only went out at night, Brilliant said, stroking the dog's coat, Miracle is his name, you just told me, Samson, yes, how could I forget so quickly, Miracle, yes, and you, Brilliant, you said your name is Brilliant, can you remind me where we met, it was before your deployment, Brilliant said, a long time ago, in a fishermen's tavern, we were good friends, remember, I would write on the walls, my novel, my oral novel, I don't do that anymore, it's a drag to have to settle down and stop graffitiing walls but here I am, a nurse's assistant and soon I'll be a nurse, I'm a responsible man and Samson soon I'll have some big news to share with you, what did you just say, Samson asked, a bit haggard, can you speak slower so I can remember what you say, you know that I went back to school, I've got a bright a future ahead of me, what was I saying, what future, can you remind

me what I was telling you, the young veteran asked, I get
lost, words make a strange noise in my head, I have epilepsy,
you know, if you could see my wound, it's an honourable
injury, you can't see it under my hair, my hair has grown
since I left the military hospital, but it's an honourable injury
and I was awarded a medal because I saved a comrade from
dying in the explosion, I held him against me, I was supposed to get married but the wedding has been delayed,
my fiancée says she's waiting for my faculties to return, as
I was saying, the attacks, the nightmares, I wake up screaming, how could a woman live with me, I love my fiancée,
we were about to, hey, tell me again what happened to me
in Afghanistan, I don't remember any of it, they told me I
woke up with a hole in my head and couldn't speak and
since then the wound has healed over, remind me where
we met, you and I, and really your name is Bryan Brilliant,
you see how quickly I forget, how could my fiancée live
with a man like me, she can't, so we're going to wait until
the fall, it's too bad because I love my fiancée very much
but she's patient and she'll wait for me, the seizures will go
away, the doctor at the military hospital told me, he told
me I've made enough progress to live on my own now but
my parents took me back in with Miracle, where would I
be without him, see, I remembered his name this time,
Miracle, even saying the words makes a strange sound in
my head, I never remember the address of my parents'
house but Miracle always brings me right there, I know the
house is near the port because my father is a fisherman, the
port is on the Atlantic, I remember that too, I see friends at
the port who've lost an arm, a foot, so I'm lucky, on such
warm evenings near the water, in the company of Samson
and his dog, Brilliant felt an urge to confide in him, Samson,

you can take off your glasses now, evening has come, why do you worry yourself so much, I have a hole in my head too, my mother, the mayor, she always said I was a numb-skull, it'll work out though, you'll see, you'll recover and then you'll remember too many things, like me, I think she whacked me over the head once too often, that's why I'm broken too, right, and when she wasn't beating me herself she'd have my Black nanny beat me with a stick, which explains my head being a little wracked, yes, mine, ah, why should that matter to you, Samson, it happened in New Orleans, when I was a delinquent, a kid, before the devasta-tion, the first one, I saw lots of things, I lost my Black brother in the water, my nanny's son, I always forgave her because deep down under the tyranny she was only following my mother's orders, and I can still see the billowing blue overalls and him at the bottom as the wave rose and garbage and debris swelled in the water, you see Samson, it's better not to remember, but Samson's expression was distant, his face had a dreamy look and he didn't seem to hear anything of what Brilliant was saying, the waves, he said out of the blue, the waves make a lot of noise, before, before I left to go over there, I don't think they were so loud, oh, too much noise, the shrapnel, the explosions, what a racket, if you only knew, tell me your name again, Brilliant, yeah, that's it, we have to go home, Miracle and I, it's dangerous here, good night Brilliant, see you tomorrow, don't forget to tell me your name when we meet, and their silhouettes disap-peared into the confines of their night, Miracle the German shepherd leaping ahead of his master as if to try and rouse some joy in him, but it wasn't even noon, Brilliant thought, and Samson and his dog Miracle were nowhere to be seen, their bench was empty and thinking of them Brilliant was overwhelmed by sadness, what if Samson never did get his mind and his memory back, his life a broken thread after Afghanistan, his friend no longer looked like the boy he'd known two years earlier, before his tour of duty so far away, Brilliant had not thought about Samson much and felt bad for forgetting him but everything around him was so bright, the sky, the sea, and he had Misha obediently trotting alongside him toward Pelican Beach, there's a time to love your friends, Brilliant said to Misha, do you hear me, Misha, are you thirsty, you're panting, don't worry, I'll give you a drink, that's it, Brilliant said, there's a time to love them and a time to lose them, and in his fetid solitude the Young Man remembered a car ride in the country in his father's Chevrolet, he was sixteen and just learning to drive, the Young Man was driving fast and recklessly in the summer sun, he was dressed in a white t-shirt, shorts, he remembered a sign planted near the woods, *They are Anti-White*, it read, come, young men, to the Klan initiation, we have a church too, a school, come, young men, we're waiting for you, the Klan set-up against the Blacks was pretty basic, it was said, a church, a humble chapel where mothers and their children prayed, and a hut that served as a school and that was called the Klan Initiation School, there a twelve-year-old student was reciting his lesson, saying that Black and white children should live separately, that they should be segregated because Black people have always been a threat to whites and like homosexuality it's a sin and the Klan would punish sinners, they should be punished, the boy reciting these words seemed to be an ordinary child and the Klan director who welcomed the Young Man seemed equally ordinary, he looked like a businessman, he was dressed in a suit despite the heat, and the Young Man noticed a peculiar

insignia on his tie, the collar of his shirt was stiff and
squeezed the director's neck and the Young Man had been
impressed when he saw him, quite normal and conventional,
the director said to the Young Man, come, you charming
boy, how did you find us, we are persecuted so we try to
be discreet, that's why we're a ways away from the city
though we attract quite a few children and we teach them
our truth, for our truth is the only truth, it is right and just,
I've been the director of our modest group, the Klan, for
several years, but always in secret, we avoid those first letters that might tip off the police and anyone looking for us,
will you stay for our fire ceremony tonight, we burn the
cross and dance around it as it burns, it represents our
offering to God, but it's very discreet because of those who
want to silence us and especially prevent us from expressing our beliefs, our truth, come, Young Man, follow me, you
must have seen the burning cross at many of our campaigns
even if adversity has taught us to work discreetly, and in an
agitated, exalted state the Young Man attended the fire
ceremony, and while the enormous cross was burning, the
cross was huge, the men, women, and children crowded
around the blaze had put on white robes, the costume of
the Klan, of their oldest incarnation, the hoods over their
heads had slits so they were able to see and to judge, and
didn't the Young Man see the crazed scene through the
flames, it was as if the cross was burning right in front of
him in his cell, burning before his eyes, yes, he thought,
that had been the day, the night of his initiation, the director
had shaken his hand and said that's good, why don't you
come and spend a few days at the camp so we can proceed
safely, we trust you, we are confident that you will cooper-
ate, he said, it was a done deal, nothing more and nothing

less, and from that day on the Young Man was one of the members of a secret society that worked its magic on him, that cross is holy to us, said the director of the smallest of the Dens, we'll show you where it used to blaze when the Klan was powerful, oh, with their paltry huts, their churches equally pitiful, with the parishioners wailing their wild orations because they are no more than savages, don't they remind you of the last Indians of our tribes, we must burn our cross on their lands so that our race triumphs, the only race beloved of God, but come and see our camp, dear Young Man, we have swings for the toddlers and you can have something to drink on a hot day like this, and as the children played they recited lessons they didn't quite seem to grasp, for none of us is born with hate, and even the Young Man thought how before that day, he'd never experienced the joy of hating, though possibly he'd been naturally inclined to such loathing and had never realized it, and the notion filled his scrawny chest with pride, and all the while the director of the Den, a man of modest appearance, he could have been a salesman in a shop, offered him further instruction in violence, no charge, he said, he showed him a shooting range where you could mow down cardboard figures with a rifle, it's only practice, the director said, for you to learn that you can kill men, women, and children without feeling, we're not keen on anything too emotional here, we'd rather be effective than emotional, how much training had he undergone there, the Young Man wondered, how many lessons had he learned that fugitive summer at the camp where little girls laughed as they played on the swings and the boys shot cardboard figures with their revolvers, and the Young Man acted innocent, he didn't want to attract any blame or be admonished by his parents, after his time with the Klan he would hide in the basement, focused on his plans, he had been taught hatred and the hatred was consuming him, wasn't that the way it had been, thought the Young Man as he paced in his cell, there, in the basement, as the leader of the smallest of the Dens had suggested, he was a man no one knew anything about, that was where the Young Man wrote his first manifesto of hate, immediately posting it on the internet, you'll see, the director said, nothing spreads faster than hatred or contempt and you'll have many, many friends, but as he paced in his cell the Young Man also remembered teenagers waving at him on the highway, he was driving so fast, their signs that said *STAY AWAY FROM THIS GODFORSAKEN PLACE, CHILDREN, STAY AWAY, LOVE ONE ANOTHER, LOVE, NOT HATE,* the word love irritated him to no end because he was in the throes of excitement with his new mission, he would have been about sixteen, he had just learned to drive, and he was the leader of the White Supremacist Youth, wasn't that what the benevolent camp director had appointed him, or would appoint him, the director reaching under his starched collar and the fold of his tie to unpin the special insignia that set him apart, yes, the Young Man thought in the midst of his insomnia, the unbearable burden of not sleeping, when he had the vision of someone rushing at him with a knife at his throat, was that Pastor Anna's son or was it her brother, or the young man who had comforted his mother, the memory was always in him, the young man with his lips pinched tight, the one who longed to avenge the death of his sister or brother coming at him and saying, you filthy white man, I'll have your skin, you'll never have a good night's sleep again, I'll rip your guts out, yes, I'm getting closer, I'm here, first I want to slit your throat, my sister was jogging in the park with friends and you were dreaming of abducting her, fantasizing about rape and pillage, of carnage in our churches, the Young Man shivered with cold but no, no one was around, a guard was stationed upstairs, he was probably armed, the Young Man thought, and Pastor Anna's son or maybe her brother disappeared in a fog, the Young Man could no longer see him, these waking nightmares were happening more and more, he thought, it was the cold of the cell or the frantic feeling of being incarcerated day and night, at the children's camp there had been hardly any talk of killing but the Young Man heard the words echoing everywhere for him, the refrain of his hatred and rage, the camp director, in an unctuous voice, the voice of a grim merchant buying young souls for his demonic market, the director who in his teachings spoke rather of a slow exter- mination, not a suppression but a purge of the people rebelling against the Order of Truth, his language was poetic and flowery and on Sundays they watched films, or maybe reconstructions of ritual films, they watched the parade of children of the only master, the one who started the slow but necessary elimination for us, you mustn't say anything to anyone, it's a secret between you and me, the point of our showing you these films could be misconstrued, they might make it out to be satanic when it's only a matter of purification, of cleansing what is soiled, you are so young and this took place in another century but for our associa- tion time is a constant, what goes on is a continuing story of forced purification, we have the same principles, the Dens and the entire Klan, everyone listen to the Supreme Wizard, or to the innumerable masters, wherever they are, and around 1920 the Wizard created the Parade of Supreme Youth, of the Aryan race, look at these youth on the screen,

boys ten to eighteen years old, at seventeen they'll be con-
scripted into the army and the girls will be devoting themselves to their duties as wives and mothers to serve their
country, both the boys and girls have had a solid athletic
education, look at their muscles, and isn't this parade for
the Supreme Wizard orderly and peaceful, he called them
his children, and as he greeted them with his salute he
would tell them of singular and utter authority over the
world, my children, be lithe as greyhounds, as hard as
leather, and let your hearts be made of steel, for you will
have much to suffer, and then, before the ceremony of fire
and the giant cross, the director invited the Young Man to
pray in his chapel, remember, he said, that this cross was
erected in front of churches, temples burning along the
roads across the South, remember, I will remember, the
Young Man promised, the smell of fire clung to his nostrils
and his hair, which would be shaved off, the director said,
I will shave it myself, but the Young Man refused to have
his hair touched and the director noted his insubordination,
what you must understand, he said, is that distinction
between us is unacceptable, even in vanity our rules are
strict, you must give yourself completely over, come with
me to this private room where we keep films from the past,
for us the activities of the present or the past are the same,
our purge is the same one carried out by other masters
whose law we follow, and in one of the films from the past
the Young Man saw synagogues burned down, businesses
destroyed, he saw men and women imprisoned, we have a
private militia, the director said, we can infiltrate any place,
we have nights of purging at bawdy houses where young
people engage in degenerate play, we shut down these
forbidden sites, we impose our strict behaviour everywhere,

we stamp out immorality, whatever is unlike us, the noble race, the one and only, for immorality, said the masters of old, the masters whose rules we follow, immorality is a social gangrene, a pestilential existence we must be rid of, so when you see the flare of this cross, our cross, think of us, and know that you are one of our children, you are the future of our Klan, yes, its future, but the Young Man was only half-listening to the director's words, only vaguely aware, and after the director mentioned shaving his head, he no longer attended the clandestine meetings in the woods, he would not be one of those ugly skinheads, his mind was too full of fire in the turbulent summer wind, he could smell the burning, the smoke on his clothes, he had learned from the Klan sites online that several Black houses in one village had burned and others would follow and he remembered thinking that he didn't like the smell of the smoke, it seemed as though the flesh of men, women, and children was mingled in it, yes, that's what it was, and the Young Man felt as if he alone was the perpetrator of his crimes, his purge at New Hope Methodist Church, the idea was his, by his actions he had made himself the lone young master, surpassing the primary institutions, the lesser Klans, the Dens and their mercantile directors, only he would be praised for his idea, the Young Man went to bathe his face in the yellow water at the sink, he wanted to be clean when everything around him was filthy but look at the scummy water flowing into the sink, he thought, what we eat is disgusting too, he'd demand of the guard that they transfer him to another cell, though he'd heard that the cells of death-row inmates weren't uncomfortable, so no, he wouldn't ask the guard for anything, death row was only a few steps away they said, and he was worried that the other inmates were trying to scare him, they made fun of him as they passed him in the shower, they said you're getting closer, on death row they even give you perfume or at least scented soap, you'll be happy there, you virginal piece of shit, go on, you're a little girl playing at murder, tell yourself you were a good shot, how many, sixteen, twenty at a time, and the Young Man curled up on his cot and pulled the grey sheet over his head, alone at last, he thought, alone even though the walls oozed with the other prisoners' shouts, did you think you would see them in heaven, that your victims would be there waiting for you, is that what you thought, the voices repeated until the Young Man fell asleep amidst the lacerating shouts and screams, Miles Davis, Robbie said to Petites Cendres, is that Miles Davis, music in the distance, the musicians and the Black Ancestral Choir will be there, Eureka will sing her psalms and she will cry out for joy, Angel, Angel, hear the voice of the Lord, Angel, Angel, wake up, today is the day of your resurrection and the angels have brought out their trumpets, listen, Angel, Angel, my heart, do you hear, I wanted to be like him, Robbie said, his skin was almost the same colour as mine, I don't play the trumpet but I can hum the melody, up on stage with Yinn, more than anything I envied him his striped suits, the languid trumpet he leaned on his hip, his night-blue blazers and the printed scarves underneath, the black socks and booties, I loved his calculated coolness, how subtle it was, how stylish, come on, get up, Mabel, we're nearly at Pelican Beach, I can hear the music too, Mabel said, she was walking faster now, it's heavy, it's too heavy, you two aren't thinking of my knees, my legs aren't what they used to be, and you, Jerry, stop pecking at my neck, look up ahead, it's amazing, the sea, the sky, barely a breeze, yes, Jerry echoed in answer, turning around on Mabel's shoulder, the sea, the sky, yes, Mabel repeated, if I had known the bag would be so heavy I'd have let Lena know, it's heavy, it's too heavy, why are you slowing down, Robbie asked Petites Cendres, they're expecting us at noon, yes, because a bell is going to ring in the sky, Mabel said, that's the way it is, you have to be on time, oh, if I had my spry young legs, Mabel complained, though now she was walking at the same pace as Robbie and Petites Cendres, she even seemed to be getting stronger, when I travelled with Fatalité, I watched some champion surfers, yes, when we went to the clubs in California, in the morning, dishevelled after a sleepless night, we would rush to the ocean, one time a man was watching us from the terrace of his mansion, he was a twenty-year-old master surfer, he looked like a golden sculpture lit by the setting sun, he had a great build and a cherubic face, he was a jet-ski champion too, a millionaire prince with a catamaran and at least twenty surfboards, he was supposed to surf in an international contest soon, and he would win, he had only one goal, to be the best surfer in the world, he spent the winter surfing in Hawaii, that's big wave season there, and the beaches are white sand, did you know that the waves can be up to twenty feet high, it's all about knowing how to land without the wave swallowing you up forever, that's how it was, and me, I was bored of living with Fatalité and going out only at night, I always had dark circles under my eyes, and I thought, that's the man, there's the husband I need, my skin would get a golden glow like his, that's what I thought, Robbie said, you'd leave me for a husband, Petites Cendres replied, you'd do that to a friend like me, and Petites Cendres' doleful voice pulled Robbie out of his daydream, after the evening shows I always get marriage proposals, Robbie said proudly, Yinn is married to Jason, but since I no longer have a daddy I get loads of marriage proposals, Robbie said, but alas we are only foraging bees in danger of extinction, Petites Cendres, one day our honey will dry up and Yinn will replace us with Cheng, his Chinese protégé, or the Louisiana Diva, so a healthy, chubby husband would be a comfort to me, and as for you, Petites Cendres, and Robbie fell silent, holding his breath, you mean that our days together are numbered, Petites Cendres said, annoyed, admit that's what you meant, Robbie, I didn't say that, Robbie said, no, but you had the flu and you didn't tell me about it, I'm angry that you're losing weight and that you're spending too much time lying around in your hammock, it's time to be strong, to rise up, we should go to San Francisco with Yinn, you're getting hot in the sun, eh, you're dripping sweat, you wear out too quickly, why should I lose you like we lost Angel, why should I accept that, Petites Cendres, be brave, come with us, resist, don't just give in and think everything will be better, life is life, always and to the end, Angel proved that, you're so obnoxious with your silences and your secrets, will you come with us, there'll be thousands of us, thousands, I can hear the music, Eureka's voice is so powerful it soars above the choir's and wherever Angel is, sound asleep, surely he'll wake up and hear it, Mabel said, the pelicans will be sunning themselves on the beach, they're starting to fly near us, too bad I'm so thirsty, Mabel said, always so thirsty, it's always like that in the summer, and this bag is so heavy, you're both young, you can't understand, you can't keep getting up on stage to dance and sing until you're a hundred years old, Robbie said, the oldest of the queens still has it, the one they call the Courtesan, the matriarch, yeah, and when she sings, god, those lyrics, back when we made love, when we were happy, when she lets loose with the nostalgia, it's like my soul splits open, I'm afraid she'll die on stage in the middle of her act, but then I listen and tell myself that'll be me thirty years from now, will I be as beautiful as the Courtesan is, her deep voice, so sensual, warm as the sun is today, and yet I'd rather have a husband, young, vigorous, someone who loves flowers, who'll ask me to come live with him at his farm in the mountains in Alaska, the glacial sky, white clouds, you're dreaming, Petites Cendres said, you belong to Yinn, to the company, you belong to the night, to the dancing, you belong to us, Petites Cendres said jealously, the Porte du Baiser Saloon can't live without you, Robbie, you belong to the Acacia Gardens, to Yinn, to me, Petites Cendres was stammering, and he was going to add, you know that my days are numbered just like Angel's were, but he stopped because Robbie had started to laugh, the grotesque character was staggering about nearby, why is that guy still around, Robbie said, him and his entourage, why are they following us, the one leading the way seemed not to have a head, his head was a red balloon floating in the air, he was waving his short arms histrionically and ranting, we'll get them, weapon up, we will get them, hey, you, young man, you must bow down before me for behind this foolish guise I am the god of money and you in your feminine frippery, you are rascals, despicable queens I would trample under my boots, hey, Mabel asked, who are these people and where are they going, they're insolent clowns, Robbie replied, and their headless leader most of all, his head is a big red balloon and they're drunk and I don't know where they came from, Robbie said, let's hurry, we'll be late and we'll miss the champagne, from my banquet of drunkenness and lust I could rule the world, the headless man said, for the world is so insignificant a thing you can rule over it without a clue what you're doing, what you're saying, but no one was listening to him, Petites Cendres felt disgusted, inexplicably, the horror he felt was all out of proportion, he thought back to the group of young men booing and catcalling as Yinn danced onstage at the Saloon that night, he had wanted so much to toss them out into the street, but Geisha, willowy Geisha in her feather corset, had thrown them out, their foolishness and their taunts, we don't need you here, she said, dragging them one by one to the stairs, and both Yinn and Cheng were unbothered, dancing and singing, Petites Cendres thought, as if the attacks hadn't affected them, at the end of the night the Louisiana Diva had sung her provocative plaint lasciviously as she always did at the end of the night, uninhibited and caustic, but this time what was provocative was what she had around her neck, below a cascade of starry jewels she wore a metal necklace so high it looked like a collar or a snare coiled up to her chin, like an iron clamped around the neck of a slave, one of those collars that sliced and bloodied those who were to be sold at a market or in a public square, the provocation was deliberate, her abasement had pained Petites Cendres, as if the cuff had been around his own neck, and more so the Diva's lament, the future is now but isn't the past always there even when we forget it, the way she laughed, the Diva's dolorous crooning neither reassured nor comforted Petites Cendres, though he admired the extent to which dissent was innate for Yinn's new disciples, even when they didn't say a word, like Cheng, or when they were hilarious, like the Black African Louisiana Diva in her wriggling glory, they knew how to express their militancy as well as Robbie did, as if their rebellion sprang from their imagination, from their art, and that same night when Cheng came on, Petites Cendres was stopped in his tracks, in the midst of the heckling, Cheng danced across the stage, not trembling for a second, was she reinventing herself after her second adoption by Yinn, the first having been by the North American family who had rescued her from life on the street in a village in China, even though she was a boy she'd been wrapped in swaddling clothes and left to die of cold and hunger out on the street with the infant girls abandoned to that medieval fate, and the kind couple, not caring whether she was a girl or a boy, adopted her, and later when she met Yinn she really came into her own, Petites Cendres thought, Yinn called her his Prince of Asia and introduced her to the rapture of dancing and singing, and on the stage, in her art, she found a measure of peace to soften the cruelty of her abandonment, though she could never forget the disgrace of having been abandoned at birth, she could never forget the young mother, so ashamed, no doubt a teenager cast out by her parents, laying her baby on the cobbles, it was snowing, it was raining, the child wouldn't stop crying as all the while the girls in the street were dying of hunger and cold, Cheng couldn't shake the thought, she told Yinn, and even though that suffering, those memories were imprinted into her flesh, Yinn taught her distance, how to let the bad luck slide, and she seemed to reinvent herself, she danced almost without moving, her serene face marked with only the slightest sign of pain, an imperceptible gesture of insubordination, if you knew what to look for, she moved toward the audience, eyes shut, eyelids thinly lined in blue, her eyebrows smooth shadows, and the bottom half of her face, the lips under her straight nose were covered in makeup the colour of metal, her closed lips and tight smile suggesting that language was non-existent, cut off, not a word, although under the makeup Cheng felt everything even if some earlier censorship seemed to forbid it, Petites Cendres spent a long time contemplating Cheng and the Diva before heading down to the street, how fruity the streets smelled, the bars open until the wee hours, there was such a warmth, people eating late on the restaurant terraces, it revived him, he thought of himself as a dying man who was in good health but maybe he was wrong, the premise was flawed, he was so easily seduced by the noises of life, he tugged out the laces of his sandals to place his bare feet on the carpet of red petals on the sidewalk, he was all about drawn-out concessions to sensuality, he thought, Yinn had freed him from the labour of prostitution and now he would never dare beg a pinch of powder from some straggler yawning up against a lamppost, no, even if someone offered he wouldn't dare, the high flame of his passion for Yinn still burned, but the fire was less overpowering, quieter, he thought, and Brilliant asked Misha if he remembered Mardi Gras before the second devastation, did Misha remember, everyone trussed up in red plumage, the masks with terrifying teeth, you need to have fun while there's time the musicians shouted as they filed through the brightly lit streets with their instruments, Brilliant and Misha ate so well in those days, the smell of hot doughnuts and café au lait, crab fritters over green tomatoes, we would stop during the parade to have tea or daiquiris, we savoured Creole dishes so we had energy to dance, dance, yes, the first day, the first night, second day, second night, we danced again, and then, just then, where had it come from, it started

to rain, a cold, heavy rain, how did it start to rain while I
was dancing and I thought you were right there, I thought
I was holding your leash but Misha you weren't there anymore, where were you, I wouldn't see you again for so long,
I'd probably had too many daiquiris but how could I possibly find you in the crowd and we were drenched, that
rain, we kept wanting one last dance, the red and mauve
feathers on the costumes disintegrating in the storm, its
violence, where were we running to, and soon after, in a
few hours, I would see my Black brother, my nanny's son,
struggling under the planks, the straps of his blue overalls
barely above the water but he couldn't swim, he didn't know
how to swim, and Brilliant thought he might cry at the
memory but he must not cry, at noon he would tell them
his happy news, they wouldn't believe it, what had Samson
said on the bench, his eyes hidden behind his sunglasses,
you know, Brilliant, if you do your duty as a soldier then
you have to kill, what I didn't know was that you never
forget, you relive the same thing thousands of times and
you think, hey, he was young like me, who knows what
future he might have had, how many more years he had
left and what he might have become, and you can never
forget because you keep repeating the moment, like you're
trying to erase a terrible mistake that will never be erased,
no, never, and Samson continued to ramble on in front of
the sea, how strange, he said, his head wound had healed,
but it hurt day and night, wasn't it odd, every wave coming
in off the ocean was too loud, too bright, they crashed and
crashed against his temples, against his face, a flogging, he
said, to the point that he was losing his mind, good thing
Samson had his dog, Brilliant thought, Miracle was always
near him, reassuring him, the German shepherd was a

lodestar, dog of mercy, his noble animal brother leading Samson everywhere, away from the bleak and fraught road of war, always forward to that light on the water, the water that Samson hated now, adrift in his madness, he used to swim every day under the same sun that now filled him with confused memories of combat, ghosts, guilt-ridden meanderings that gradually ate away at Samson's conscience, shrouding the light of the outside world and especially the dazzling light of the sun, it was as if the sun had gone over to the darkness, Brilliant thought, it had become its own opposite for this soldier full of remorse and who could only explain himself to himself, because like Victoire the world hailed him as a hero, where was everyone so that he could tell them his news, Brilliant thought, Kim, Rafael, Jérôme the African, the two dogs Damien and Max, he would bring them before him, they seemed so frail under their blankets on the hazy beach when Brilliant brought them something warm to eat at night, eat up, Brilliant would say, I know you're hungry, this is from the kitchen of the Café Español where I work in the morning, here are some more blankets to stop you shaking from the cold, on those nights in November, December, January, when Brilliant watched over them, when Fleur was back from touring in Europe, even Fleur's mother didn't know, Kim and Fleur were living on the street, you could hear Fleur playing the flute and Kim drumming, and when Fleur was in Rome Kim had sent him a photo of her daughter, this is Pearl Saved from the Waters, she's a year old, this is my daughter, but Kim, proud Kim, received no answer, not a word, no, from Fleur there was only a haughty silence, Kim said, he didn't love her anymore, he'd forgotten her in the blinding rush of his success as a musician and composer, and what else, Brilliant thought, he no longer wrote to his mother either, Martha was invisible, so far away, out of mind, it was as if Fleur had warned everyone not to come near, and the guru Rafael, busy with his crafts and his illicit wares, took fierce Kim back in, she felt safe and satisfied at Rafael's house, didn't she, Rafael had too many women, and children too, children of every colour, he always said the house was his Noah's ark, and Rafael dreamed of buying a boat for them to live in, they would be out at sea more often and it would make his trade easier too, though he was wary of the coast guard and the informers keeping an eye on him, they knew too much, but Rafael was smart, he didn't have a criminal record yet, he went about openly, yes, that's how it was, Brilliant thought, Fleur didn't say anything to Kim and now it was too late for her to confess her love to him, what a loss, Brilliant thought, Misha looked up at Brilliant, he seemed to be listening, Brilliant leaned down toward Misha, saying, you remember, don't you, Misha, don't you remember, or were you at the vet's recovering from the second devastation, you too, you were absent for so long, even though Kim had confessed her love to Fleur once, she'd left him a message on his phone, it was Clara he had always loved, ever since they had played together in that concert in New York City when they were small, he only had eyes for her, Clara, two virtuosic children bound by music, their bond was stronger than anything else, and Kim, his ashen-faced street friend with the filthy boots, the woman who rummaged through dumpsters with him, who had slept with him and the dogs on the beach those nights when the sea was so rough, the wind twisting out pines and palm trees by the roots, theirs was such a different love, what tied them to each other was the pity you feel for an animal, Kim had been Fleur's foundling, but the mist was so thick at night Brilliant could no longer see where they were, on what beach, he had to lean into the wind, their voices disappearing into the night and as they made their way alongside the water, on Atlantic Boulevard Brilliant held Misha's leash slack in his hand and Misha barked at a police officer on horseback about to cross the road, horse and rider were heading toward the centre of the town, what's going on, Brilliant asked the cop, whose face was protected by the shield of his riot helmet, there's still fighting at the demonstrations in front of city hall, the policeman said solemnly, pulling up his horse, he said, I was off duty and now I've been called back in, I was with my wife at our golf club and my phone rang, it's so aggra- vating, it rings day and night, we never get to rest like everybody else, the policeman said, there were two rallies happening in front of city hall, one was a group of aging skinheads, though it would be more accurate to call them Nazis, the policeman knew them well, as time went by they looked more and more like cavemen in their threadbare brown clothes, the others were peaceful protesters denounc- ing the ideology of the first group, that's what the policeman said, with sticks and pocket knives, another protest that's gonna turn violent, the policeman explained, someone will be spending the night in prison, gotta go, let's go, the police- man told his horse, it's too bad because I was off duty, the violence never stops, the policeman said, never stops, but Brilliant and Misha were moving away to the cool shade beneath the palm trees by the sea, and Adrien asked Simon if he could move the lunch table closer to the beach even though Simon had already told him that he couldn't, Mr. Adrien, you and your friend would be right by the rising waves, and I don't want to get my shoes wet serving you such a tasty lunch, here's the wine list, Simon said, while you wait for madame you may choose one of our new wines, or at least peruse the list for your pleasure, it's not yet noon, is it, Adrien asked Simon, looking at his watch, our meeting is at noon, Adrien thought about Charly dropping him off in front of the lobby of the Grand Hotel, she had to meet one of her clients at the airport, she was so serious, so devoted to her work, to her clients, Adrien thought, and he laughed at what Dorothea had said to him that morning after he woke, you'll be having breakfast with the young lady who pretends to be your chauffeur because she does your shopping, so impudent, this young woman who only has old men for clients isn't for you, Adrien, not for you, no, but Dorothea you're forgetting, Adrien replied, ruffled, it's my birthday today, Dorothea was increasingly getting on his nerves with her reflections and her indiscretions, it was unbearable, I've told you, Adrien went on, although today I am ninety-five, well, perhaps a bit older, but don't think of me as an old man, I will never be an old man, Dorothea, any more than my friend Isaac is, never, Adrien insisted, with all due respect, Adrien, I'm telling you anyway, this young lady, as attractive as she is, will cause you a lot of trouble and who knows, Dorothea said as she helped Adrien with his cane and his hat, I may not be around to defend you anymore, and Adrien left his maid standing there, he'd taught her to read and write over the past few months, grumbling with impatience at times, he didn't like that she had such a predilection for religious texts, he'd left and slammed the door shut behind him, Charly waiting for him in his black car to drive him to the Grand Hotel, she'd promised that they would meet up at noon and have lunch together, could Adrien request that Simon, his regular waiter, give them a table as close to the sea as possible, it was so hot today, Charly asked in that charming voice of hers that made Adrien quiver in his beige linen suit, and out on the Atlantic coast it was nearly noon and Charly in her chauffeur's uniform, her wavy hair tucked under her cap, was nowhere to be seen, she was late, Adrien thought, opening a book on his lap as Simon set some red orchids on the table, there won't be too much noise today, will there, on my special day, Adrien said, more as a command than a question, but Simon, rather than reassuring him, told him it would be a particularly raucous day though not so close to the sea, no, higher up, on the terraces and in the village halls, there are several weddings today, Simon explained, same-sex couples really love a June wedding, we have a couple, two men, getting married, they're very sweet, a smidge old in my opinion for the trials of marriage although I don't know, I have no interest in being married and I'll be thirty soon, and a couple of girls are marrying too, they're on the young side, and you think they'll make a lot of noise, Adrien asked, as if he felt ill at the thought of such activity, such vitality around him, they'll be happy, the lot of them will be happy, Simon said simply, and, as if he'd thought it over for a moment, Adrien said, skeptically, if you have a partner is it really necessary to marry, look, I've had friends who lived together for forty years without getting married, I'd go so far as to say they never thought about it at all, well, perhaps marriage wasn't for them, Mr. Adrien, otherwise they would marry, as people do these days, even those whose relationships are not yet sanctioned by law, maybe because those laws are stupid and futile, Simon said, shouldn't the world be recreated each and every day, Adrien hesitated but then said, no, no, of course not, looking like a wise old man with his hat, his face a little pink from the sun, people your age say reinvent the world, he was about to add, and oh, you are all so tiresome, the weddings, the noise, the joy, how I hate it, he muttered without forming the words, remembering that his wife Suzanne must be out there somewhere, somewhere in that perfect landscape, warning him to say no more, she was like Simon, for them the world was made new every day, his wife had always been the daring one, always ahead of him, evolving, moving into the future, she was such a free spirit, Adrien thought, how could I have misunderstood her so completely, he watched as a young couple passed by his table with their lunch in a basket, they were relaxed and having fun, preparing to lay a white tablecloth on the sand and take out bottles of wine and some fruit from their picnic basket and sit on the beach in their bathing suits, and Adrien asked, offended, are they allowed to have lunch like that on the sand so close to my table, and Simon replied, again not reassuring him, that on this beach everything was allowed, it's unfortunate they don't allow dogs and cats and roosters and chickens like they used to, though at the hotel next door, which isn't as fancy, it's all allowed, it's rather pleasant, Simon said, and looking up at the sky, he added, we still have herons and egrets, they visit us every day, but iguanas are forbidden, we don't let them nest in the trees because our customers complain, why don't you get married, Adrien asked abruptly, the girls seem to like you a lot, that's not a reason to get married, Simon replied categorically, you see, Mr. Adrien, I am single by choice, so that I can concentrate on the hospitality business, I must advance my career, I started out as a bellboy at the Grand Hotel and here I am at your table, it's an honour for me, Mr. Adrien, and Simon fell silent, pointing out a great blue heron in flight, what a beautiful day it is for you when one of our great blue herons flies away like that, such majesty, I'll keep climbing up the ladder, one step at a time, Mr. Isaac, our venerated boss, won't always be around, don't count on him dying, Adrien said, as if Simon's words had pierced his own heart, he's still around and will be for a while, he's like an oak, and dying would be too mundane for him, he never does anything like anyone else, and as he bantered with Simon with a kind of familiar vanity, quite aware of how preposterous he was being, Adrien saw that the young couple, rather than having lunch on the white tablecloth, were necking, the girl leaning eagerly over the young man and kissing his mouth greedily, once more he would have to ask Simon if he could move the table for his lunch with Charly to avoid the indecency of the scene and what would surely follow, but Simon's gaze was turned away, he was staring at the young couple and Adrien didn't ask him anything, he saw in a spark of memory the couple he and Suzanne had been, perfect, it was as if he had been standing before a Manet painting, time had stopped and he thought of those lunches on the grass he and Suzanne had shared when they were young and beautiful, two poets about to burst onto the literary scene, all those lunches on the beach, the same wine, the same fruit, and the same basket in which they kept their meal warm, he who could only really appreciate art by incorporating himself into it in the most subjectively carnal way, he wasn't a connoisseur like Jean-Mathieu, studying what was cold in a painting, what was white, the trembling of mist on figures in some maritime scene, the characters cowering in a storm under the floating rock of a black sky that looked more like crustaceans than they did human figures, but Adrien felt Manet had painted *Déjeuner sur l'herbe* just for him, unfolding like a lifetime of picnic lunches on the sand or on the grass in parks and gardens, endless relaxing hours with Suzanne, Suzanne in the white dress she used to wear, reaching for a plate where patches of shadow would soon be strewn on the white tablecloth beneath the autumn leaves, still green, no doubt that's how it was for the lovers meeting for lunch, though what held so much beauty in his memory was probably a banal event for the couple so clearly besotted here before him, a moment by the sea in which their bond was transforming, as if they were as hungry for each other as for the meal laid out and waiting on the white tablecloth, yes, Adrien thought, and, noticing that Simon was no longer nearby, he dozed off and saw his father approaching, his father presenting himself humbly but with the shadow of a mocking smile, it seemed incredible that his father was so young while Adrien was getting older and older, his forehead wrinkled, though he was a handsome man, as Dorothea used to say, his father daring to appear out of his astonishing perpetuity, where everything was eternally green, meadows and men, he thought, and Adrien said to his father, dear father, I didn't call you, why are you here, dear father, you cannot come and take me because I am not ready, and Adrien jerked awake because beneath his hat he felt like he was melting in the sun, with a wave of his hand he dismissed the night-mare of his father insisting he come with him, intruder, Adrien thought, what does he know, standing there staring at me, he's so smug, where is Charly, why is she so late, we'll have to move the table, the waves, the sun, he thought, Simon is right, there's too much going on in this spot, we should move the table under the trees, yes, it should be moved, Adrien thought, and the Young Man remembered what the chaplain had told him, the chaplain didn't approve of capital punishment even for the worst criminals, no, all men were his brothers, the Young Man listened with a frown, doubting his sincerity, because if that was true what was he doing in the prison, this Chaplain of the Chamber of Execution, no doubt, the Young Man thought, he had some morbid relationship with the executioners, the men who at the appointed hour would flip the switch and send electricity coursing through his body or plunge a lethal cocktail into his veins, don't make faces like that, the chaplain repeated, the psychologist and the lawyer and I are trying, as we do for numerous prisoners in solitary, not only to have your sentence reduced due to mental illness but for you to be able to walk outside in the courtyard once a week, between the four concrete walls of the courtyard, you can't even see the sky through the bars of a window, no, but you'd be able to start exercising once a week and it would take you out of the dark night of your cell, the night of the mind in particular, nothing healthy or good can come of that, you're carrying too much of a burden, hatred is insidious when it takes root in a young body like yours, it spreads, rotting everything, it destroys the brain, it's a cancer, and the Young Man thought, if they're giving me an hour a week, even in the courtyard between four concrete walls with no view of the outside, if I am granted this privilege it's probably because my trial is approaching and they want me to be able to stand in court, they don't want to have to have to carry me in because I refuse to eat their garbage, they want to inject me with the strength I'm losing and then inject me with their poison, but the chaplain's gentle voice was louder than the Young Man's thoughts, the chaplain saying listen to me, and listen to your lawyer too, he can't help you or even get the sentence that's about to be handed down reduced if you keep acting up like this, throwing your meals on the ground or even in your guards' faces, we're used to bad behaviour but these things will have serious consequences for you, are you not afraid of death, listen to me, I've been able to save a number of the condemned these last few years by begging for a pardon from the governor or by writing to the Office of the Pardon Attorney, but for some time now no one has been responding to our requests for clemency, they're not interested in listening to us, or they don't hear us anymore, and the executions will go on one after another, even the Supreme Court no longer supports our appeals, everyone around me is recommending this most awful punishment for you, they believe your crimes are racist, shocking, so I beg you, help me see the death penalty abolished for you and others like you, I remember a thirty-five-year-old woman who was executed, she'd committed her murders with a partner, they were both on heroin, and her lawyer and I asked for life in prison rather than death by lethal injection, yes, I'd made the request as if I was asking her parents but there was no mercy, everything was turned down and it pains me every day, of the four hundred people in the country on death row there hadn't been a woman executed for years, the last time it happened was a century ago, it's an exceedingly rare thing, and Carla Eva was executed before my eyes, she had converted, the expression on her face was open, imploring, she looked innocent to the end, was asking life to forgive her for crimes she couldn't even recall, God tricks immature souls by imposing such unconscious burdens on them, and the Young Man had stopped smirking and he listened to the chaplain's words, thinking, after Carla Eva it will be my turn, his hands shook, they were sweaty and dirty because there was filth all around him, Carla Eva's atonement would be his hell, and the Young Man shouted at the chaplain, go away, I don't want to see you anymore, you're a liar, you were there when she died, I'm sure of it, and you blessed her, you used Carla Eva for an experiment like a guinea pig, when the jolt of the injection bucked her chest you were there with your sacraments and your prayers, as she passed from one hell to another you were there, chaplain of name-less agonies, agonies of condemnation, she had no funeral, only a mass grave, she had nothing, no respect, go, I don't want to see you anymore, we'll meet again, the chaplain told the Young Man, I understand your anger, but for the first time don't you feel some compassion, for yourself as much as for this woman, yes, we shall meet again, the chaplain repeated, I've had enough, Mabel said, of the cru-cifixions every day in Detroit, in Chicago, in New Orleans, I've had enough of these white policemen killing my people, sons and grandsons of my blood, they nail them to the ground or in the dusty streets and kill them in cold blood when they haven't done anything, nothing at all, they're little Black delinquents, that's all, they're murdered for a stolen cigarette, and the children's fathers, they're murdered too and I weep over their graves, may God hear me, their graves are fresh, these crimes are fresh, so terribly recent, and the bodies of the dead groan and wail, may the Lord hear me, yes, may the Lord hear me, yes, will He always be deaf to our cries, Mabel said, dragging her bag behind her, and Petites Cendres put his arm around Mabel's waist and walked slowly with her, listen Mabel, you know, when I came for my four o'clock visits Angel never confided in me except to tell me Brilliant would watch over Misha forever and then he would ask if Misha would know how to find him among the comets after he ventured into space, an astronaut with no possibility of return, would Misha find him after his interplanetary journey, though Angel did also tell me that he remembered how he and Lena had left their hometown, it was so fast, they packed their stuff in the car in one day, he was still at school and a couple of students and their mother had assaulted him, you are not going to infect my daughter, my son, no, you are going to leave this school, this town, you and your mother, even when they were in the car the screams kept welling up around them, go, we don't want your virus, we don't want you or your mother here, go away, they left in an uproar of indignation and hatred, and one evening a group of people with AIDS was walking behind them, they were walking behind their car just as they were about to stop at a motel for the night and these men and women, who were suffering, they said to Angel's mother, we are with you, we are with you, see how they treat us, we are less than human to them, they were skinny, emaciated, and yet they were still standing, they were coming out of hospitals where they weren't wanted either and they walked with Lena and Angel and it was like a procession of pain, that's what Angel told me, Angel, who confided little about the past, he told me everything that day, he must have had a fever, I had to put a cold compress on his forehead and I didn't see him after that, at four o'clock he'd be asleep, he was sleeping a lot, Misha by his side, it seemed all he could do was sleep, even when Dr. Dieudonné arrived to give him his injection, even when Eureka came to rock him in her big arms, he seemed to be sound asleep and calm at last, Petites Cendres said, may the

Lord of men hear me, Mabel repeated, they could be my
sons and my grandsons, why does my daughter keep having
children only for them to be tomorrow's martyrs, why, Mabel
asked, Reverend Ézéchielle paid for my plane ticket so I
could see the baby, Mabel said more joyfully, he was a
bawling, screaming boy, healthy, I was so proud, we're getting there, Robbie said, that's Eureka's voice we hear, she
sings like Sarah Vaughan, when I was up on stage with Yinn
I could imitate that voice and others too, I used to wear
dangling earrings and a low-cut white top, maybe they'll be
singing the whole repertory of the Black Ancestral Choir,
Benny Golson, Art Farmer, like in the sixties in Chicago,
except their voices will soar out over the waves, fly far, far
away, Robbie said, look, a colony of pelicans, we're almost
there, Robbie said, we have nothing left, no more bottled
water, Mabel said, but you know I won't let you go thirsty,
Robbie said, I always hide one or two, they warm up quickly
in my jeans but I have lots of pockets, and Mabel explained
that it wasn't for her but for Jerry, she took a sip from the
bottle Robbie handed her and said, yes, the water is warm
but Jerry will be very happy, eh Jerry, Mabel said to her
parrot, letting the bird drink from a makeshift cup made of
cardboard, look at those pelicans landing so unhurried on
the shore, but they're so fast when they fish, Robbie said,
as Petites Cendres watched the constellation of punks following them, they've been behind us there for an hour,
Petites Cendres said, you mean the man whose head is a
red balloon, that joker, and those other jokers with him, the
headless attract the headless, Robbie said, don't look at
them, they don't deserve your attention, Robbie said, but
they scare me, Petites Cendres said, yeah, that guy with a
balloon for a head, maybe we should worry about him,

there have always been punks like that, hypocritical and repressive, but he's only a man with an empty head, just a mannequin, maybe he's not even human, flailing his arms around while he spews inanities, and at the boy with the red knee-high boots too, the trapeze artist, the acrobat will light himself on fire tonight with the flames of his hoop, he's saying, the jackass is saying that he'll spread the blaze wherever he goes, even though you can't see his head you can hear him snickering, and Mabel looked out and saw a boat that seemed to be lurching on the water in the rippling light, it's a cruise ship from Holland, Mabel said, so far away, a boat as big as a city and carrying people, there are swells all around the dinghies, they're so small on the ocean that no one seems to see them, there are families on those boats, whole families, they're raising their arms up in the air and waving, I don't think the cruise ship captain can see them from so far away, no, otherwise the little boats would be tied up to the fancy ship, right, there's a dance or a ball tonight on that ship, they have them all the time, even during the day, the lights are twinkling from afar, yes, all the time, Mabel said, when Jerry and me sell my ginger beer and lemonade at night on the wharf I can hear them, I can hear waltz music coming from the ship, the music and the choppy sound of the waves, Mabel said, we're getting closer, that's the Black Ancestral Choir you hear, Mabel, it's just that my bag is very heavy, who would have thought, Mabel said, eh, who would have believed it, he had no meat on his bones at the end, Mabel, you have to remember, Petites Cendres said, that it was right there, on Pelican Beach, this deserted beach, that Angel loved to come and play and run with Misha, in those days when he could run with Misha, this was the beach of his happiness, of Angel's joy, that's why we're headed there, said Petites Cendres, you'll stop complaining about your knees and your feet here because this is the beach of Angel's freedom, he'll be leaving from here on his interplanetary journey, to his chosen planet, like he always wanted, Petites Cendres said, he told his mother he wanted to take off for his planet from this beach, a planet that will remain unknown to us forever, Petites Cendres said, I had no idea it was so far from my place, Mabel said, oh, if I had known, Lena and Lucia will be coming in Brilliant's car, because finally he has a car, and Brilliant will take Misha for the long walk to Pelican Beach, Petites Cendres said, and we'll be reunited for the procession, a great procession for our friend Angel, Robbie said, so Mabel, stop complaining about your knees, your feet, no, stop, once you're in the sea you'll be able to put down your burden and you'll see, your bag will be so light that it will hurt, it's so much effort, true, but when your bag is less heavy it'll hurt more, there will be a sailor waiting for us in his boat, we've reached the port, Robbie said, and in the yard, which was as the chaplain had described it, a fairly large courtyard surrounded by windowless cement walls, the Young Man was prowling around awkwardly even though the guard had been told to take off his handcuffs for the regulation hour-long break, for the Young Man to get his exercise, and the guard watched him, leaning against the wall with guns hanging from his belt, and on the other side of a barred door a second prisoner was waiting for his turn, hey kid, he shouted to the Young Man, we have the same slot on the same day, hurry up, breathe the air and smell the flowers so it can be my turn to wander around, you know I haven't spoken to a soul for days, I'm in solitary like you, though for different reasons, I'm not the one who'll end up on the gallows, nah, I'll be in this hole another twenty years, and you want to know why, because I had a damn good life, I sold drugs to rich students, lawyers, the well-to-do who never deny themselves anything, and I lost everything, a great life, I had mansions and money, but I got caught, too bad, I had a sailboat too, a fine boat, my wife visited on Sunday and she managed to slip me some quality pharmaceuticals, I could have made some mixes for my friends, I could have taught you how, bits of paper passed from one cell to another, even sticking it up my ass, but they saw everything, they knew, and so they put me in solitary, you hear me boy, I've got another month to go, I'm losing my mind but keeping my cool, I have to, I'm the boss, the smuggler king, I get the goods, whatever, you don't get it, you're not listening, take a deep breath as you wait for the flowers in your tiny square garden there, remind yourself that your luck won't last, they'll come to escort you away and you won't know the day or the hour, could be tomorrow or in thirty years like it was for many others, but for you, boy, I hear it'll be faster, so will you stop standing around and staring up at how high your cage is, get out of there, if you don't want to walk or toss a ball against the wall then hurry up, I need some down time, what are you doing, boy, pondering your future, your rosy future, I'm Kevin, the inmate said, I'm the boss here, everyone respects me, white or Black or gang leaders, everyone respects me here, the man said, as he let the Young Man take in the muscular build of his chest and arms, I'm not scared of anyone, he said, but the Young Man wasn't looking at the prisoner named Kevin, he started to walk in circles the pale light streaming into the yard where he was a captive in a numbered uniform, the neon light seemed to streak white

bars on the fabric of his orange suit, all he could do was
turn and turn in infernal circles from which he knew there
would be no escape, with the words of the chaplain he'd
heard that morning ricocheting in his head, begging him to
come to his chapel, with the guard, of course, I once worked
in a prison a ways from here, the chaplain said, no doubt
looking to convert him, the Young Man thought, in San
Quentin, a prison where I was surrounded by the most
hardened criminals and we called the convicts there dead
men walking, that's what they were called, the convicts on
death row, those unfortunate men, Sister Christina, my assistant, she was a sensitive woman, it could be she was too
sensitive to the prisoners' fates, she and I became attached
to one of the criminals, he'd converted, not to any religion,
though, he'd discovered he was a writer, but too late, alas,
he was a talented poet, gifted, his talent helped rehabilitate
him and the poems he wrote were eventually published,
he was the author of thousands of verses of surprising
power, poems expressing his condition as a maximum-
security inmate and his unbearable regrets and remorse, but
also his desire to reform, he told us that he'd been touched
by grace and that we needed to forgive him, though he was
relentlessly reminded of his repulsive crime, he had robbed
an eighty-five-year-old woman and murdered her in her
own home, he was granted no clemency but Sister Christina
and I pleaded for a pardon because he was consumed by
repentance, this poet, this murderer–writer, he wasn't like
most of the others, he had a soul, he was aware in his grief
of the harm he had done to his victim, he cried every day
and every night, Sister Christina dedicated herself to having
his books published, but the whole time, the closer he was
to the chamber, despite his books and the critics' admiration

for his talent born in torment, the court refused to grant him a stay, their answer being that even though this man could write a lovely poem, it was too late, the victim's family was inconsolable to the end, Sister Christina said that the family of the condemned man was against capital punishment and appealed to the compassion of the court, the murderer–writer had been incarcerated for almost twenty years but he was refused clemency, whether by the governor or the pardon office, no one other than Sister Christina and me seemed to have any compassion, I keep hearing his voice like an echo, the voice of the repentant prisoner, saying, I will have neither future nor family, never, no hope, I will die at one minute past twelve o'clock and you will hear my muffled sighs but it will be too late, it will be too late, I shall have only unspeakable regret for the woman I killed, a piano teacher, alone at home and waiting for her students, I did that, and gradually Sister Christina became his friend, his confidant, yes, she was his friend for many years, the one who transformed the morals of a murderer, the one who recited the writer's poems to the judges, reading in a wavering voice how much he missed the time when he could hear wind in the leaves, a breeze in the whispering of voices and my mother saying, go now, go, it's time to sleep, child, and here I am struggling between agony and the hubris of not dying, unable to ask for help from anyone, I weep as I think of the path of wrongs I have travelled, *hush, hush*, child, it's time to sleep, I'll be there, inconsolable, in the chamber at a minute past twelve, inconsolable, *hush, hush*, child, it's time to sleep, but I'll find her, her, the woman at the piano, and she'll tell me at last you are forgiven, *hush, hush*, child, it is time to sleep, they'll light a candle for you, hold me, you from whom I received the cup

of forgiveness and of love, he had received that cup of love
and forgiveness from Sister Christina, and I remember, the
chaplain said to the Young Man, at one minute past twelve
o'clock you could hear the wind in the leaves and the blue
sky turned black, he whose childhood had been wrecked
by his parents' abuse, his mother had been an alcoholic and
his father beat him, whipped him until he bled, lay at forty-
eight years of age on his deathbed, not breathing at one
minute past twelve, Sister Christina and I had failed to save
him, no, right up until the very last mercy had been denied,
and the Young Man continued to walk in circles, shivers
coursing through him as he remembered the words of the
chaplain, he had dreamed, he who hardly slept to avoid the
nightmares that left him gasping, he barely slept, hovering
on the surface of slumber then waking in a panic, he had
dreamed, the nightmare relentless, that he saw one of Pastor
Anna's sons or he would see the son whose mother had
been one of his victims at New Hope Methodist, the avenging son, who would lead him to a dank corner of the prison
and force him to sit on a chair, he would bind his feet and
hands, that was it, he was holding something in his hand,
either an axe or a stone, he could feel his shadow, the
shadow of the son standing behind him, would he slit his
throat, would he cut off his head, the Young Man would
wake up alone in his cell, there was no one there, crying
out, it's not fair, as if pleading for the mercy of the man
avenging himself upon him for the murder of a mother, a
sister, and his vengeance would be absolute and pitiless,
and the Young Man turned and turned in the airless courtyard as Kevin the inmate yelled, when are you getting out
of there, your time is up, do you want me to come rip your
balls out if you have any, and that was the nightmare of his

sordid reality, his waking hours, walking around and around without being able to leave his damned circle or the four concrete walls, the Young Man knew he should be afraid of the inmate called Kevin, tattooed head to toe, a skull on his chest, and screaming obscenities at him, and the Young Man thought of the writer–murderer, the one who had written poetry, the sweet, sentimental one who killed an old woman in her kitchen and then covered her with a sheet, who had even taken the time to make himself an omelette and a coffee at the scene of the crime, he died with honour, the Young Man thought, yes, despite his conversion to poetry, he didn't capitulate or turn himself over, he was, like me, a killer, poetry was his weakness and yes, the Young Man thought, his salvation too, yet these words troubled him, come, child, it's time to sleep, come, child, the leaves are singing in the wind, and hearing the voice of the chaplain who'd repeated those words like a dirge, if he'd had any tears left the Young Man would have cried, and as Daniel was walking Mai's dogs, the two Labs that looked so much like their mother, she'd been such a loyal dog, the Labrador they'd had for years and whom Augustino loved so much that he'd never understood why she couldn't live as long as him, that the old dog wouldn't be with him his whole life, that Augustino would outlive her, had caused his son fits of grief that his parents could only counter with paltry words, that's how it is, animals, like humans, are on earth only for a short, unpredictable time, the sad lesson was neither acceptable nor satisfactory for Augustino, who cried and rejected his parents' attempt at comfort, and Daniel, remembering this, Augustino's first moment of defiance, stopped to visit Stephen more frequently than usual while walking Mai's dogs, no doubt because Daniel had met the delicate young writer Henri in Scotland and was aware of his suicidal tendencies, where Eddy cut the cord, the ripcord so to speak, at the hotel where the writers were staying during the international festival, after he'd met Henri, a former bestselling author now betrayed and forgotten and whom Daniel compared to Stephen, to the frailty of the writer in Stephen, but where Henri had been a writer lucky with women and money and whose fortune had dried up when his erotica stopped selling, Stephen was a lonely young author looking for a companion, and he thought he had found one in José, the humanitarian chef, Stephen embodied the stereotype of the solitary writer with all its contradictions, wanting to be with someone and wanting to be as alone as possible in the house that had been loaned to him to write in, Charles and Frédéric's house, entrusted to emerging writers as a legacy of immaterial value and as an affirmation of the treasures that would ensue from their creative spirits, Stephen didn't doubt for a second that he was such a treasure, a creative spirit, his first book, *Demons*, had finally been published and, to Stephen's dismay, was now the property of the world at large, but Stephen, who disdained the company of girls, secretaries and agents, quite unlike Henri when his books had been selling, when he was young and frivolous, a writer too much in the limelight and now shunned to the point where he wanted to kill himself, who regretted the frivolity of days when he could have been writing real literature, when he could have been a serious author, Stephen, for his part, was ensconced at Charles and Frédéric's house with too many men and boys, because there, he told Daniel, the residue of José's island nights on the road, Stephen was no longer alone, José always had too many young people to cook for on the street, people

who came over to wrap up the night and slept on the terraces at the front or at the back of the house like they did
on the street, it had to stop or he would break up with José
or tell him to leave, wasn't it so much like it had been in
another time, said Stephen, when Charles would grow impa-
tient with Frédéric always in the company of destitute young
Black men right out of prison or reform school and not
knowing where else to bring them but home, Frédéric, the
man they called the Black man's lawyer even though he
was simply a musician, a painter, an artist with a gracious
heart, there you go, Charles said, it's insane, the whole town
is at our door and soon I won't be able to write in peace
in my room, in my office, I can't, and unflappable as he
always was, Frédéric listened and then said that these children of Grégoire's, of his old Haitian friend, the refugee,
they needed him, they needed his financial support and
they had such a big house, why didn't they open it up to
others who didn't even have a roof over their heads, and
Charles would get angry, infuriated at Frédéric's sweeping
gestures of kindness that disregarded his own comforts,
lawyer for poor Blacks indeed, Frédéric, why don't you put
your music first, weren't you writing a quintet, what's going
to happen with that, yet another project that's going to get
shelved, in the end, Frédéric, you'll achieve nothing as usual,
and what a pity that is, Charles said to Frédéric, infatuated
with his own independence, with his projects and whims,
is this how a gifted man like you wastes his time, and Daniel
was convinced he heard phantom notes on the piano, what
would the quintet have been like, was he hearing the first
draft, Daniel knew that even in searching for the best and
most ideal partner in the world, Stephen would pry himself
away from José, who was so devoted to everyone but

himself, Stephen, those men, the boys whom he thought of as not yet fully formed, stretching their legs in the living room, strolling in, far too relaxed in their shorts as if they'd just come in from the water, Stephen, who had his prejudices, told Daniel that these men only talked about their addictions, about alcohol and drugs, they didn't wash, didn't cut their hair, none of them had a trade, as charming as some of them were, they were losers, Charles would have been shocked, as he'd been when he lived with Frédéric and had to put up with the shiftless brotherhood sprawled about his living room amid his books and his art, above all he'd been scandalized by their talk about cocaine, heroin, referring back to the great masters of psychological thrills, the discoverers of hitherto unheard-of paradises such as those Timothy Leary had introduced generations ago to thousands of people who hadn't understood that magical invention LSD, which could allow those in the know to access a cosmic life that could be glimpsed down on earth, the blazing hues of another world that was easy to reach, for the afterlife was no further away than within ourselves, these young men said, as they passed through Charles and Frédéric's house, but what weren't they telling, these drifters, Stephen said to Daniel, they had to be chased away, they couldn't sleep in the house anymore, didn't you take LSD yourself, Daniel asked, didn't you tell me that you took some with a philosopher friend a long time ago, when you were in university, oh, Stephen replied, that was a very long time ago, now a bit of hash at night is enough for me, as they say, you can't be a teenager all your life and now that my book is out and it's been well received, even if I feel uneasy about it, I feel very exposed, it can be hard for an author, for any author, it might be time to start writing a second book, in silence, yes, in silence, and Daniel, I won't even mention how sexually promiscuous José's delinquents are, several are prostitutes, they go to the baths, I won't tell you how much it bothers me, though José doesn't seem to be fazed by their behaviour at all, he says he's there to offer them meals, that's it, Daniel listened to Stephen, they were in the same garden beneath the acacias where Frédéric used to smoke his cigarettes, one after another, his face reflected back in the mirror against the landscape of palm trees and bougainvillea, and wondered if Stephen saw multiple versions of Eli in José's kids, all of them invading the house just as Eli used to do when he came in through an open window in the middle of the night, they were Eli's messengers, they had the innocence of his blue eyes, they came and went with the same detachment, full of a mischievous sexuality, which was why Stephen had undoubtedly started to fear them, Daniel thought, and then, soon after his breakup with José, who had done him nothing but good but whom Stephen had repudiated when he saw him on the street as if he were Eli, Stephen found himself so alone and unable to write that he would go out late at night, out to the bars, and come midnight Stephen's long silhouette roamed the deserted streets, with that prematurely hunched back he'd had since he had written his book about Eli, as if he carried Eli on his shoulders while writing his story, and during one of those outings to the bar, he later confessed to Daniel in amazement, he had had an epiphany, yes, he would write a biography of Charles, he would be among Charles's many biographers, or perhaps of Charles and Frédéric, I was on my seventh gin and tonic when I had this revelation from heaven, yes, and I seemed so drunk that they wanted to throw me out of the bar, but I wasn't,

I was simply free of Eli, that was it, Stephen told Daniel, it was a night of triumph and liberation because Charles and Frédéric were alive in me and what am I doing in their house if I can't write about their works and their lives together, yes, I understood this with a flash, I was leaving behind my slough of despond, to put it that way, and on my way home I saw a man and a woman bickering, the woman said to the man, is it my fault if I drank too much, I'm going home with you anyway, I can't do anything else, and he grunted uncharitably, this is always how it ends when we go out, I hate you, you ugly pumpkin, I hate you, woman, and Stephen said I felt such pity for the woman that I helped her as she was about to collapse on the side-walk in despair and tried to reassure her, telling her that her husband loved her in spite of everything, yes, he loved her, and she was so far gone that all she could do was say again and again, every night, every night he insults me, oh, young man, I won't be with him for much longer, here, I'll get up, let me hold your hand, may the good Lord of pau-pers bless you, and after comforting the poor drunk woman, Stephen, exhilarated, had been able to return home inspired by his new literary project, it seemed to him that as the sky grew light his soul was clearing up, why was he so full of doubt when, now that he was on his own, he was such a happy man, Stephen wondered as he ran a hand through his tangled hair, why did he always doubt everything, Adrien was making revisions in pencil in the fourth version of his Faust and then afterwards in pen, did he know, as much as even Goethe or Berlioz had, why this ugly character had sold his soul to the devil, to satisfy his insatiable appetite, of course, but was this clear cause for damnation, his want-ing to feast on knowledge, too, was it a crime to want to improve your intellectual knowledge, Adrien mused beneath the brim of his hat, bobbing his head before closing his eyes to the sun, why had Dorothea not allowed him to bring his computer, she'd said Adrien would leave it somewhere or lose it, moreover, Dorothea said, a pen and a notebook will fit in the inside pocket of your suit, Mr. Adrien, and you won't lose them, that woman and her advice are too mixed up in my private life, Adrien thought, but we can't live without one another, now she knows how to read and write, and if that's what I've accomplished on this earth the here-after will be dazzling for me, I'll no longer have any debt to Him, or to Her, the Eternal Mother who follows us, what a fraud, but who was that standing in front of him, wasn't that Charly, her face seemed drawn below her chauffeur's cap, I've come to settle accounts, Charly said impassively, her voice almost cold, oh, you want us to discuss my poem "Taking Account," it's overdramatic, isn't it, I couldn't stop fussing with it and I botched it, or I think I did, I'll ask Dorothea if it's still in the trash, sometimes I retrieve things after I've thrown them away, I'm like many of my poet friends that way, what ineptitude lies on the road to perfec-tion, *n'est-ce pas*, I've come to settle accounts, Charly repeated, I was your driver for several years and the time has come for my salary, what salary, Adrien asked anxiously, I've paid you every week, you know I'm a man of my word, I have no more to give you, all I have is my pension as a former literature teacher at a girls' school, nothing else, it's been decided that I'm leaving everything to my children, they know that already, even my lazy mathematician son with his head in the clouds, he was Suzanne's favourite, so there it is, I have nothing else to give, Adrien woke with a start, his watch read one minute past twelve o'clock, it was

12:01 and Charly wasn't there yet, Simon appeared and told Adrien, we're in the waves, we have to go higher, in the shade of that pine tree there, Mr. Adrien, don't you feel the waves at your feet, Mr. Adrien, no, nothing, I feel nothing, a few drops of warm water from the sea, but that's all, Adrien 'spoke with difficulty, he picked up his hat and his cane, there's a hill over there, you'll be better there than under the blazing noon sun, Simon said, I'll take the table and chairs, don't worry, Mr. Adrien, it's not noon yet, it's a minute past twelve, Adrien said, go ahead of me, my dear Simon, I'll follow, I am following you, you see it was time for my nap, no, the twelve-year-old suicide bomber would not kill anyone today, neither in the market nor on a bus, no, no one, the man with the cart and the tired donkey had come, he'd come to relieve her of the belt with the glittering bells, but wouldn't they explode as soon as a finger slipped in to try and prevent the blast, no, she wouldn't kill anyone, she had fled to the purple mountain and on the other side of a barbed-wire fence her parents and her younger sisters were waiting for her in a refugee camp, no, she wouldn't kill anyone today, yesterday it was Jerusalem, a sixteen-year-old suicide bomber, Ayat, was on her way to martyrdom, it happened in a restaurant, what to do with the hundred and forty wounded left behind in the wake of Ayat, the human bomb, what to do with those wounded, what a long list there was of child suicide bombers waiting to spill their blood, but the twelve-year-old suicide bomber would not be among them, no, she thought, our nation is angry and defiant, I know, she thought, after our history of humiliation and revenge, that the sole dignity for my people is death, dying to redeem the humiliation, that's what I know, I was told that after powerlessness, after constant defeat, the enemy must be vanquished, the enemy is everywhere, I am told, everywhere, there are so many conflicts but I want no more than to live, to see my parents and sisters on the other side of the barbed wire, it's dawn and they're so far away, Ayat would have been married this summer, she would have been a wife and mother, Ayat, shattered flesh, the suicide bomber followed a rough path up the purple mountain, the peasant and the donkey and the cart advancing painfully, what is it, my child, what can I do for you, the man said, are you hungry, are you thirsty, here is my donkey to carry you if your feet are bleeding in your sandals, where did you come from, the camp is over there, you see, but it's quite far, but your parents and your sisters are waiting for you there and tonight you will rest by their side, how much longer can you walk like that, every passing second sounds the alarm thought the kamikaze bomber, and for her too, Wafa, the one whose head was wrapped in a turban, Wafa, who was called the Joan of Arc of Palestine, what would be found of her but flaming pieces of flesh, no, I will not kill anyone today, thought the twelve-year-old suicide bomber, there's the sky above the purple mountain and they are there waiting for me at the camp, my parents, my sisters, still there thinking our daughter will soon be with us, the peasant, the donkey, the cart, where were they, were they the last silhouettes she could make out against the sun, between the trees, was this it, was this the final reckoning, and what were the celestial rewards promised to the Palestinian Joan of Arc and to Ayat, who would have been married in the summer, when they were living girls, what did they imagine that could be more beautiful than this earth, more heavenly than life, what did they imagine, tricking themselves into believing in some secular paradise invented by men and for men, this is what the twelve-year-old suicide bomber was thinking as she walked farther from the promised reward of her sacrifice, all she wanted was to see her parents, to kiss them, to see them, but every second she could hear her belt, and if they so crave a paradise where they can rape virgins why don't they make martyrs of themselves, why don't the men who inflicted this belt on me, this barbaric duty, why don't they offer themselves up for this implosion to their heaven, why us and not them, this is how they dominate us, how they reduce us to the greatest humiliation, to die for them and their hollow words we set ourselves aflame with the light of our own lives, I ask these children, thought the twelve-year-old suicide bomber, to come back and walk with me as we file up the purple mountain, let us be together in a chain, holding hands, a chain to save our lives, for here is the merciful sky and the sun on the purple mountain and soon like me they will see their parents and their sisters again, because on this day, alongside the man with the cart, the donkey, wouldn't it be wiser to live than to die, even if the alarm bells are chiming on my belt, even though my heart is beating too loudly, it's too loud, and Mai listened to the waves lifting Samuel's boat, the *Southern Light*, as she sat by the mast watching her mother at the helm of the sailboat again moving placidly, calmly, you could hardly hear the wind in the sails, Mai thought, she wasn't perfect like Mélanie was and probably never would be, although her generation was competitive, they were too proud to have to compare themselves to anyone else, better this conceit, Mai thought, the illusion that they were born all-knowing, with the gift of prophecy, perhaps believing they owed it to themselves to hurry up and live while they could, they wanted to shine

brighter than everyone else, and above all they were mate-
rialists, they wanted the latest electronics, they wanted
market value quickly spent, Mai thought, and this was probably the beginning of the end for Tammy, she had received
so much, but nothing of value, neither love nor affection,
only things, goods, glinting blue roller skates that lit up, a
car, tablets, games, a glut of gifts, always more, replaced as
fashion demanded, fashion accelerating to the point of glut-
tony, every day we were full and we wanted more milk,
always more, but the soul remained empty, rasping and
empty, Tammy was wearing those blue light-up roller skates
when she said, I want to go with you to Manuel's, there's a
big party tonight and his dad will be giving out ecstasy, I
need some antidepressants, I missed my exam and I just
want to feel better, you understand, Mai, I know you do, I
know that you tried some with Manuel, you and Manuel
aren't afraid of anything, and tranqs always make me feel
good, I was wearing my fancy roller skates too, Mai thought,
and I was guiding Tammy through the night, come, come
with me, we'll go party at Manuel's, at his father's place on
the beach, it's the most charming property on the island,
the most elegant, I don't get why my parents won't let me
see Manuel or his father, they won't let me go over to his
house, no, I don't get it, I can manage on my own without
them except that I promised my grandmother Esther that
I'd come home to give her a kiss before midnight and to
listen to some music with her, to read her a chapter, Tammy
and I would chat in the evening as pink and purple shades
danced on the seawater, we would go around on our roller
skates, and I think that was the beginning of the end for
Tammy, before she stopped eating, before, yes, other girls
and boys from school had been invited to their house too,

their mansion, there was always competition, Manuel's father travelled a lot, to Russia, to Israel, his business was booming and this time he'd just come back from Colombia when he took us in, at the party there were several students, they came from all over, after dinner we'd go swimming in the ocean and there would be dancing on the beach, there would be what Manuel called a Ship of Ecstasy and those pills for just a few pennies each, a rave, we could stay up and dance all night, and then there was Manuel and me, our bodies hot against each other, tripping out, the soothing hallucinations, our parents long forgotten, we were alone in the world at last, he and I, each of us alone with our own elixir of happiness and wanting nothing more, don't take too much, Manuel's father said, and while we were dancing together, Manuel and I, so close it was as if our bodies were one, fit and tanned, his breath burning against my cheek, Manuel's father, flashlight in his hand, came up to us and said, not so long ago I was like the two of you, enjoy your youth, it's over so quickly, now come down to dance on the beach, your friends are waiting, and who was always near us but little Tammy, Tammy who no one asked to dance, I don't know how many pills she took that night, she fell asleep on the beach and I went to wake her, I asked her why she had missed the exam, but she couldn't remember the school or the date of the exam, I think it was in chemistry, she whispered, I had to wake her up several times, don't bother me, she said, that's where I'm at, she said, my goal is perfection, yes, and that word, perfection, I started to hate it, it was the word that would make Tammy sick, languishing in bed at the clinic, that's the word, Mai thought, and that's why I don't want to be perfect like my mother is, like my grandmother was, wasting away from hunger, my friend Tammy always compared us to each other, girls, she said, look at my big breasts, my big knees, you see I'm not as delicate as you are, I know you see it, I can't escape my defective body, I'll always be blamed for what I am, the girl I am, a girl who's always hungry, I eat a lot, you see, and I knew that was the end of Tammy, I knew it that night, at that party, I knew it but I said, come with me, let's go to Manuel's house, we'll have a good time, come on, my parents told me not to but that's how it is, I'm old enough not to have to listen to my parents and you don't have to listen to yours either, Tammy, my grandmama Esther, whom I adored, was in the guesthouse waiting for me, I was supposed to come in before midnight, I knew that but it was so much easier to forget when I was dancing with Manuel, our faces pressed together and the breeze coming off the sea, we danced like that late into the night, today with my mother our expedition to the Invincible Fortress has been a success, the sea turtles will be released, the veterinary teacher and his students will carry them over the waves shouting with joy, today was a perfect day, I will tell my mother, a triumph aboard the *Southern Light*, because you see, Mama, this is also what perfection can be, don't you see, Mama, Mai thought, and Suzannah had written to her friends that morning, I'm young, I have my future ahead of me, a picture of her had gone around, Suzannah in her bikini and long blond hair, you're teasing the boys her father said, you're about to find out just how I'm going punish you, you'll see and you won't do it again, and then a second video up on YouTube, the father stripping her, pulling out her hair, Suzannah's long blond hair strewn over the living room carpet and Suzannah humiliated in front of thousands of viewers, this is your punishment, the father said, I'm going to give you an old-man haircut and everyone will laugh at you and now, on this morning in June, Suzannah's mother and her two girls were huddled on a piece of grass by a ramp on the highway where a cross had been planted, it was here, on this highway, that Suzannah died in disgrace under the wheels of a truck, Suzannah's mother thought, this is where she sacrificed herself like others who throw themselves off a bridge because they feel humiliated, betrayed, more children who've been tyrannized by spineless, perverse fathers, and the little girls laid their offerings, a few toys, a doll, on the narrow patch of green by the cross, we see it all the time, Suzannah's mother thought, men who terrorize everyone with their ghastly bombs in European airports, in restaurants, cafés, but what about men like these, the father of my child, my daughter who died of shame, they're domestic terrorists, killer fathers with their good intentions and their morals, and how glad Suzannah's mother was to have left that man, to finally be separated from him, but it had taken endless beatings for her to recognize who they were living with, she and her daughters, it had taken Suzannah's immolation on the highway when she should have left him long ago, brutal man, a brutality that became significant only through her daughter's pain, as if she hadn't had time, a mother of three children, she hadn't had time to really think about him, this man, his fury, his pig-headed way of educating his daughters, and his violence against her too, the tragedy of mothers is they always think of everyone else's survival before their own, Suzannah's mother thought, she would leave three white roses on the green grass wet with dew, for you, the daughter I will never see again, you who loved to dance and sing, you wrote to your friends, I am young, I have my future before me, what your father did was like beheading his child, who is talking about them, about these men who terrorize us in our own homes, we sleep with them at night, women and mothers, our words go unheard, I'm divorced now and finally free of that murderer, but what good is my freedom to me when I've lost my oldest daughter, my hope for the future, mine, hers, we were so close, may the sun warm your little broken bones, my child, may the rains of heaven console you, pray for me that I may think of you in peace, and the sisters were asking their mother, Mommy, why is there a cross, what happened to our sister, Mommy, and Suzannah's mother didn't answer, her children were so young, she would explain to them later, she would tell them there'd been an accident, yes, a father had murdered his daughter on that highway, that's what happened, but she knew she wouldn't be able to say anything for as long as she had this stone of disaster pressing down on her chest, what you don't know, Kevin the inmate shouted to the Young Man walking in circles in the courtyard with the concrete walls, is that there are convicts on death row who have waited so long, up to ten years, twenty years, they can't wait anymore, and they beg to finally be allowed to go to sleep in the chamber no one leaves, to go and sit in the worn-out leather armchair with its belts and black straps, do you hear me, boy, we call them the volunteers, some of them are really bad men, stranglers, their specialty was catching women, raping them in the woods and then strangling them, vicious killers and rapists, but they volunteer, they're aching to go to the chair to make everything go faster, such heroes, eh, will you be among them, will you, you know you have to be fearless here, I hold my own against the gangs, I'm covered with knife scars, stigmata, get out of the goddamn courtyard before I attack you, what's sadistic is that their jailors refuse them the end they want, to fall asleep on the chair of solace, they prefer to torture the volunteers who wait for years, you, I don't think you'll wait that long, the room is ready, your funeral bed is strapped up and waiting, so come on, get out of there so I can box against the wall, you're gonna get dizzy following your own shadow like that, here comes your guard to shackle you back up, may luck be with you, boy, they don't let me out much, we'll probably never see each other again, and the Young Man heard Kevin's words without listening and followed the guard to his cell where the iron door was shut behind him, there was a panel in the barred door that was almost completely opaque, through which the Young Man received his meals, which he usually dumped out, though not this time because the guard was leaning by the door and watching him, the Young Man went to sit on his bed, disgusted by the toilet and the sink, gross things pressed up almost right against the bed, he thought, his hands and feet were numb from going around in the courtyard until he had turned into a statue, solidifying into ice as he walked, he saw himself as a child with his father, they were on the wooden balcony of their house, his father was rocking in his chair as he did every night, on the balcony there was also a wooden swing no one used, and the Young Man's father said, I will not be like my grandfather and great-grandfather, they supported segregation in this city, no, I will not be, because, my son, that was a hellish time, disgraceful, we can only feel guilt, don't forget, we must atone for incalculable sins, the private schools were exclusively for whites, there were public schools only for Blacks too, but they had to go there on foot and the schools were as miserable as the Black people's houses, damp shacks on white plantations, it will be redeemed by my children and yours, my son, don't forget, and when the first Black activists demonstrated they were shot down and their homes and their churches were burned to the ground but one day there was a mutiny, the time had come for these abused Blacks to rise up, the revolt was crushed quickly and during that riot our family also lost people, that was a long time ago, we were poor whites who could hardly read and write, but we were cruel and racist too, cruel and racist, the Young Man thought, except that they had to defend themselves against the rebellions, the riots, my great-grandparents, my father's grandparents, were they just supposed to give in to the African invasion, were they supposed to rub shoulders with those wretches, in his manifesto the Young Man renounced his father, his mother, these converts to the Black race, he rejected them, he thought, there would never be equality between whites, Blacks, and people of colour, no, never, the White Supremacist Youth would be victorious, they would reign even if it meant a struggle, let others debate, let them pontificate on television, the schools would go up in flames, and first the church where they came to pray would burn, the New Hope Methodist Church, the Young Man would take his revenge on the two joggers, the girls who had called him white boy in class, white as linen, he'd been so shy, so weak, he couldn't do it, rape them, waiting for them behind the bushes at the end of the bicycle path in the evening, no, it would have frightened him too much to touch their quivering flesh with his fingers, he couldn't do it, he was too afraid and they were so lissome, agile and silky under their white skirts, their tight black shirts, two girls against him, he was alone, it was too much, and from Berlin, from London, thought Daniel, from the various cities where Samuel was presenting his ballet *China, Slow Movement*, Daniel received a message from Samuel almost every night, we're here, Papa, sometimes the show gets rave reviews or else they hate it, people protest, there's no way my work can please everyone, we'll call you tomorrow at midnight, Veronica and Rudolph will be with me and you'll be able to see the three of us, we're inseparable during the performances, even when we're as far from New York as can be, here's a video of the show in London yesterday, tomorrow we're leaving for Germany, see the gas masks on my dancers' faces as they cycle around the stage, the white smoke on the stage, the red confetti and the swirl of the black cloud above the audience, see the slow suffocation of climate change, some people find it really disconcerting, those who prefer to ignore the present and future reality of our lives, China bogged down in a swamp of soot and coal, I am told, but not us, our children don't yet go to school wearing gas masks, no, that might happen over there, far away, but not yet at home, Papa, I see the swamp our civilization has become, its degradation in places where it's impossible to breathe and I try to counter with musical comedy so that the irony, a kind of cynical unconsciousness in which we lose ourselves a little more every day, weighs more heavily and all you can do is sit uneasily in front of the singing and dancing, it's as if we don't hear the death knell resounding beneath these shocking, upsetting tableaux, last night was an excellent performance, a young audience that seemed to get it, and our threesome travels from city to city and we always think of you and Mama, it's better for us to stay together, even if Rudolph has to make up a few days of school when he gets back, the very earth across which we travel, dragging our luggage from one airport to another, seems to tremble with violence, like an inferno always ready to belch out its flames, we're always stunned that we're able to be together when in many other families in similar circumstances, simple travellers like us, no one knows who will be killed, tonight, tomorrow, all of that, this looming uncertainty, you'll feel it in my next piece, Papa, I'm working on it with Veronica, Rudolph is having fun doing the set, it looks like the green lianas of a hanging forest, a serene, deep green landscape to restore hope, and the most fascinating music, it's like a fountain of energy that renews itself with gentler, more enchanting sounds, I'm sending you kisses, dear Papa, and now I'll let you go with just these few words about work, soon the three of us will go to sleep in our hotel, it's a relief, we're so tired, yes, it went pretty well in London tonight, dear Papa, Rudie still refuses to study dance, he's stubborn, as you know, and Daniel detected some misgivings in Samuel's words, some new apprehension, the next day he would see their three faces on the screen of his iPhone, the act of seeing so wonderful that it would be like hugging their faces, their heads appearing from some ether, from the place where thoughts were formed, his children on the screen were ephemeral but he felt more optimistic as soon as he heard the familiar voices, Rudolph would speak to him last, always joking a bit, reminding him of Augustino when he was small, his arguments, so you don't want to go to the dance studio, you always refuse, Daniel would say to him, I draw planes, Rudolph would say, I'm going to be a pilot, you'll see, Daniel, his grandson was stubborn but Daniel was too, he'd always insisted that Rudolph not call him Grandpa but Daniel, you shouldn't always bend to the habits of old age, being a grandfather and being named as such, no thanks, not for him, or for Mélanie either, it was too early, and so Rudolph treated his grandfather as if he were his older brother, perhaps it was good that Samuel had changed, he had been so happy-go-lucky, thought Daniel, remembering his son on the beach, coming home late with the same nonchalance he might have felt after going to a nightclub, it wasn't the same as when he sang with Venus in the Temple du Corail, *oh abiding joy*, when he still had that easygoing joy, his days in the sun and by the sea, untouched by drama, this child so well loved by his mother, his grandmother, Daniel thought, he'd worried that all the love would make his son an arrogant man, but wasn't it what Samuel had lived through that had changed him, it was careless for a father to forget that, Daniel thought, children live too, and they suffer, perhaps even more than their parents, even though they never say much about it, Samuel remembered the tiny oracle in the streets of New York, that thirteen-year-old sackcloth Madonna sitting among heaps of bags, a Bible open in her lap, and she spoke to him, he could hear what she had said to Daniel, what will you do, she had asked, you are vile hedonists, what will you do when these buildings and skyscrapers have collapsed, listen to what I say, for the voices speak to me and I am not mistaken, and Samuel turned to her and yelled from his convertible, shut up you lunatic, that's what you are, you're just a crazy woman, but how he regretted those words because the sackcloth Virgin was no more, like Samuel's dancer friend Tanjou, their bodies rested now under stones and fire, or stones concealing a fire that had gone out but the spark of which could never be extinguished, Samuel said to his father, even if it was flooded every day with torrential rain, that fire would burn on because it had taken hold of bodies whose consciousness was like a lamp on a torrid night, it would never go dark, who knows, even from generation to generation, for that evening, in the bright autumn light, the half-light of September mornings that seemed as if it had passed through a camera filter, a light that was not icy yet but which heralded the coming of cooler weather, yes, through that cold brightness, Samuel said, he watched as bodies dropped from the sky, and among the angels falling from the sky like snow the towers burned, and Tanjou the Pakistani student, Samuel's dancer friend, he whom Jacques had loved but rejected as soon as he got sick, Tanjou was falling, there were no strings tied to his hands or feet, and he fell steep and hard to the ground, or he'd skidded along the walls, his boots barely moving, falling in a frozen dance, there he was, Tanjou, whose brow would in a few moments be blackened by the smoke, he would close his eyes, where was he, the friend he had met at Jacques' place, the professor's, and how could Samuel not have saved him from falling, again and again he would see him from his studio window, they'd said it would be a nice day for Our Lady of the Bags too, the girl Samuel had so meanly insulted, stupid child, how many times had he said those things, she was buried beneath the towers, her Bible on her knees, praying and looking up to the indifferent sky though it was to eternity that she now raised her tearful gaze, asking, as she'd done when she'd been on the street, where am I, where am I, can you tell me, red leaves from his morning walk were still stuck to Tanjou's boots, and Samuel, watching Rudolph as he drew airplanes on his work table, would hear them again, hearing those airplanes spinning in the sky was like hearing their fiery din, it seemed to him that in his drawings Rudolph was claiming the memory of his father, remembering as he did even if he wasn't born yet, he hadn't lived it, already the memories were contained within him, he couldn't avoid the mark these events had left on his father Samuel's life, and that June morning Daniel received an email from his reporter friend Rémi, the message zipping to Daniel, blue letters that seemed to be floating as if Rémi were saying, this is an emergency, my friend, you must read this right away, Rémi told Daniel that he'd had news of his son on combat duty in Afghanistan, after a few months of fighting, his son, Ilan, had been sent to a clinic in Los Angeles, a new clinic where Vietnam vets also went, wrote Rémi, Ilan had been admitted for therapy sessions because he was suffering from post-traumatic stress, that was the term used by the psychiatrists to explain his son's agitation, everyone at the clinic had acute, worrisome symptoms, so Ilan wasn't too alone, he could talk to the others, he could share his pain, the symptoms he was experiencing, bonds of sympathy and compassion were forged between these individuals who no longer slept, who suffered irrational panic attacks or who seemed to have hardened up emotionally, they were indifferent to everything, they were seriously damaged, the psychiatrists said, and Rémi wrote to Daniel, is it true, is that what my son is, a victim of ongoing trauma he can't seem to escape, floods of tears wash him away, he hides to cry, he holds his hand over his eyes, Daniel, must I come to terms with it, the horror my son feels through some for-mulaic diagnosis in a medical journal, it's so clinical, psy-chological distress, my son, Ilan, he was always in good health, what will he be like when his mother and I see him, oh, why did I let him go, why, Daniel, I stopped working as a war correspondent to be a pacifist, I didn't want anything to do with that violence, it's so regressive, I thought that my wife, my son, and I would be safe in the country-side, it's bucolic, you know, where we live now, a few steps from the sea, our boat by the dock, among the birds, and then it hits us, this syndrome is the seed, the bad fruit of war, PTSD, I don't know when my son will recover, and my dear Daniel, if I had listened to my wife everything would have been different, I'm guilty in all of this, I'm a guilty father, so guilty, I let him go, I gave Ilan my consent, yes, I'm afraid so, I didn't want to overstep, I told myself he was already a man, he knows what he's doing, but at twenty are you, are you a man, that's what my son wanted to prove above all, that he was virile, strong, and now who is he, who will he be, please help me, dear Daniel, because I have no idea what to think anymore, my wife and I decided to ask for him to be transferred to a hospital in our area but for now they've refused, our son's behaviour is considered too violent, do you understand, Daniel, what this means to us, to his mother and me, violent, our dear Ilan, they said that was the first sign of his condition, and Daniel wrote back quickly, saying most of all we mustn't panic, my dear Rémi, Ilan will get good care and you will discover your son as he was before, because you know as I do, Rémi, that humans aren't born weak and helpless, that he can, in his desire to live with the challenges he'll face, contend with the gaping cry that our most private wounds leave in us, the ones that are the hardest to admit, the most shameful, he's ashamed of himself but he can't say it, he's reliving his war over and over, you and I, we don't know what he's done or what he saw others do, as parents we're on the outside of a war that he's wearing like a straitjacket, it undermines our ideas of peace, ideas that no doubt seemed so superficial to him, my dear Rémi, I'm thinking of you, and especially don't panic, wrote Daniel with trembling fingers on his iPhone, ah, thought the Young Man, sitting on the bed in his cell and biting his nails, finally the volunteer, the inmate who had been begging for his execution for years but who was being made to wait for his turn in the chamber, finally, after ten years of complaining, of pleading with the guards and the courts, finally they appeared to tell him one morning as he was brushing his teeth, it will be tonight at midnight, be ready, they said his name, Michael, be ready, Michael, he had been just a number like me, and the fact that they actually spoke his name like he was human aroused his suspicions, and Michael the killer thought, yes, tonight, but now I'm not ready, I want to go to the chapel, I want time to pray, he told the guard, the chaplain will be with you until the end, the guard spoke as compassionately as he ever had, you'll be able to confess, you'll have time, I didn't expect to be told today, Michael the killer said, you've waited twenty-one years for this day, the guard said, everything will be what you've hoped for so long, I asked that you not be made to wait any longer and your lawyer can do no more, wasn't this what you wanted, you graduated from Cornell, you know the law, we felt the delay was too long and that it was torturing you, you were one of the volunteers, weren't you, after university, Michael the educated man said, I went to work in an insurance company, I couldn't find anything else, and it seemed like even my face rubbed employers the wrong way, Michael remembered the students he had gone to school with, they were lovely, those students, but they didn't want me, I could never figure out why they ran away from me, they didn't like me talking to them or looking at them, Michael said, and he asked the guard, will the parents of my eight victims be there, behind the glass, yes, the parents will be there, the guard said, they've been hoping for years that you would be executed, don't forget what you did to their daughters, I did it out of frustration, because of the university students, Michael said, I couldn't resist the impulse anymore, but what I want to do tonight is to ask God, why did You make me, Lord, a criminal who raped eight young girls, why did You make me this way, obsessed, maniacal, with these satanic thoughts about sex, obsessed with raping the women who walked away from me, first mutilating them with my knife, yes, I will ask God tonight, why, Lord, You who claim to be just, why did You make me such a monster, that's what they said about me, that I was a monster, so why, God, did You make me like this, is it my fault that I'm a criminal, that's not me, I was a university student, a nice boy who one day was overwhelmed by terrifying, irresistible desires, irresistible, the criminal is You, a malevolent God, this is what I will say to God after midnight, like Christ I will say it is finished, I die, I too am on a cross, I ask no forgiveness but simply that You explain to me, God, why have You forsaken me, and why at one second after midnight shall I be nailed to the cross of the execution chamber, can You answer me, God, and the Young Man remembered Michael's testimony, the last words he had spoken to the guard, Michael repeating that he wasn't ready, no, not tonight, we'll come and dress you, the guard said, we'll take care of everything, you'll have your meal then you'll walk between us, four of us, that's the way it is, one regiment and you in the middle, you're familiar with the hallway, there's a lingering smell in the hallway to the chamber, we call it the smell of death because we can never forget the smell coming off the inmates, cold sweat, it already smells sepulchral, I don't know how to put it, but over time we've become as attached to the smell as we are to the convicts, we notice when their steps falter, the tension in their smiles, their mouths go dry, and the howls that cannot surge out of their entrails, they know as well as we do that it's too late, we pity them, it's natural, that's how it should be, we're with them for years and then look what happens, they will suffer so much that even we can't watch, we're such hard men and we can't watch, the parents who see everything from behind the glass, the parents rejoice, they'd like the condemned man to be tortured even more, they crave the revenge that pain brings, when it's over they applaud and if they're truly callous they'll even say it was too easy for him, he didn't suffer enough, he slipped so hastily to sleep, the thing is they're always thinking of their daughters, they think only of their children, they imagine them being raped and killed over and over, but us, we remember that there is a man, this man, we know him and we've been talking to him for years, a prisoner seemingly no different from the others even though he was on death row, we ended up forgetting where he was going to end up, which door, which cell, and we realize there will be no recourse, no recourse, the Young Man thought, that's how the door had closed on Michael the assassin, and Adrien thought perhaps it's time for a fourth version of my Faust, I could modernize it, he's a demagogue who can't get enough of buying the world and its inhabitants, he dreams of achieving immortality by acquiring the planet Mars, and what else, I'll make him the Grand Acquisitor of our world, scathing in his rapacity toward all of the worlds he looks upon, but his Faust wasn't that ambitious, Adrien thought, remembering how the waves under the table at lunch had lapped at his shoes, wetting the bottom of his pants, the pants Dorothea had ironed that morning, how curious that I felt nothing, is it bad circulation, numbness, dismissing the thought, Adrien looked at his watch, it was ten past twelve so where was Charly, she'd said noon, where is she then, he wondered, not without discomfort, the noon heat was overwhelming even in the shade of the pine tree where Simon had set up his chair and then, with great care, the table where he was to have lunch with Charly, Berlioz wrestled with his Faust just as I am with mine, Adrien thought, one day he'd called his work an oratorio, then it was an opera, the damnation of Faust obsessed him as it obsesses me, would there be four solo voices, a children's choir, was Faust a legend or a true story about the conceit of absolute power, why not a children's choir and an orchestra, was that too much, at one time I would have discussed this with Frédéric, Adrien thought, nodding off in the drowsiness of the summer day, what could be sweeter than giving in to sleep right by the sea, but Simon was still talking, leaning over Adrien, is everything to your liking, Mr. Adrien, he asked, I had to wake you to move your chair because a wave could have carried you away, these summer waves come on unexpectedly so we keep the children who play on the rocks at a distance, what a great loss it would be to our city if we were to lose a venerable poet like you, Mr. Adrien, swept away by a wave, I've not yet read all your books but I will during my holidays, your disappearance would be such a loss, Adrien was no longer sure whether he had dreamed Simon's flattering words or if Simon had actually spoken them, but whatever he'd said had immediately faded into the sea breeze, though there was hardly a breeze, Adrien thought, and there was

Charly walking toward him, her wavy hair tucked under her chauffeur's cap and her shiny teeth even whiter in the sun, I must regain a more dignified demeanour than this, Adrien thought, here I am flopped in my deck chair with sea water soaking my shoes, really, I should, but Charly seemed to be brimming with warmth for Adrien, typically she was not given to much affection and Adrien's instinct was to step back but he couldn't, let me kiss you, she said, come on, what are you afraid of, you say you love me, Charly's kiss was abrupt, almost aggressive, like a sting, a bite, like the sting of an insect on his cheek, on his neck, it was a bite, Adrien woke up moaning, enough, enough, the fiery sun was shining on the sea and he saw Simon walking over with a jug of water, it was as if he were approaching in a pallid mist, it might have been better if he'd done what Dorothea had recommended, Adrien thought, these sunny June days were too exhausting, he shouldn't have left the house where it was always cool, he was certain now Charly would not come, and Petites Cendres was thinking about what Dr. Lorraine had told him, she'd been a surgeon in several African countries, all it took was for three drops of blood to seep in under the glove during a surgery, that's it, the virus entering the body through a thin cut, back then they said it was just a virus, as if they were talking about a cold, some commonplace infection, we didn't know yet that thousands of Africans were dying in Lusaka, thousands, how could she begin to describe the ravages of this virus, it seemed at first to affect Africans and homosexuals in particular, hot-headed discrimination, everyone judging one another, it was in every community, perhaps what tormented me the most she said was this early manifestation of mistrust and hatred that was encouraged everywhere, even among our doctors and nurses, just like that, we were in the time of the plague, of leprosy, who hadn't seen it on television or in the newspapers, it flashed by our frightened eyes too quickly, that tragic shot of the cemetery in Lusaka, who hadn't seen that picture of gravediggers in plastic coveralls digging a pit under a tree that looks like it's been uprooted by a cyclone, and beside it a mortuary cross and the hundreds of dead in bags, men, women, like so much trash to be buried for fear of contagion, quickly covered with earth so that they could be forgotten, so that we wouldn't have to look at them anymore, women, men, children, who remembered these images, and if Dieudonné and Lorraine weren't able to save Angel their failure would stay with them, Lorraine said, there was a new drug that might help him, and who knows, Petites Cendres too and Angel's friends at the Acacia Gardens, the two African children Dr. Lorraine had brought back from Africa, soon they'd be able to return to their grandparents, yes, they were cured, Lorraine didn't say what things might be like for Petites Cendres, she hadn't said a thing, simply expressed a little hope, Petites Cendres thought that maybe he was too gullible, he believed in that chance, its glimmer was his strength, and after all Dr. Lorraine shared his guarded confidence and continued to treat patients at Dr. Dieudonné's clinic, the gravediggers from Lusaka Cemetery, on the island, would the gravediggers from the island's Cemetery of Roses take him by surprise, no, no way, Petites Cendres thought, he was growing stronger, yes, even if the improvement was temporary he would travel to the demonstration with Yinn, Robbie, and the cabaret queens, he would go with them to proclaim his right to respect, though it was really just a futile effort to please Yinn, to make Robbie happy, and how sad it would be not to visit Angel and his doves, the tame white pigeons and the turtledoves, every day at four, and as for Mabel's parrot, well, Jerry's voice was too strident, Petites Cendres could hear him squawking away on Mabel's shoulder, Mama, where's Merlin, where's Merlin, the day was getting hotter, the walk was long, and it was too much for Mabel, and for me too, Petites Cendres thought, but he was proud to be here, on this long walk along Atlantic Boulevard, yes, he was proud, we're getting closer, Robbie said again, we're getting closer, they were still being tailed by the guys with straw hats and their faces hidden behind their shark masks, some of them turning to Petites Cendres and mocking him, hey, girly boy, nice shirt, you've got a girl's shirt on, hey, you, where are you going like that, Petites Cendres didn't answer, sliding behind Robbie and Mabel and following in their footsteps as they made their way along the shore and into the coolness of the breeze, a whole colony of pelicans was flying slowly above them, the man whose head was a red balloon whistled insults around them, and Petites Cendres couldn't make out what he was saying or raving about but he was afraid, and who was that coming up to them now with his dog, could it be Brilliant and Misha, Brilliant was holding a bottle of water, before the champagne at noon, my friends, he declared, hopping along and pulling on Misha's leash, just wait and see, my friends, I have news for you, you're going to be so surprised, Lena and Lucia are on the beach over there waiting for us, they've come in my car, and Petites Cendres let his worries fade, I'm with my friends, Brilliant and Misha are here, and we have come to offer up songs for Angel, there'll be more and more of us here together and Brilliant is as animated and funny as ever, forget the gravediggers at Lusaka, that was a long time ago, not today, this is the era of progress, of metamorphosis, Yinn says ours is a revolution for the entire world, Yinn may be right, and here's Brilliant handing out water, we're so thirsty, even Misha, and what if Yinn is right, a revolution through patience and love, what if Yinn is right, Petites Cendres thought, *Southern Light, Southern Light*, words on a loop in Daniel's head, it was almost noon, Mélanie and Mai would be getting to the marina, they were probably about to moor, or they were lingering as they did among the mangroves in the islands of peace where Rémi and his family lived, perhaps they would get to see eagles flying, eaglets and hawks, and iguanas, their green heads popping up out of the sea grasses or, sky ablaze, dozing in the amorphous silence of the middle of the tropical day, and even though it was so sunny out they could hear the rumbling thunder, they'd be in port soon, free and happy, that was how Daniel imagined them, he preferred to forget the underground that inhabits us all, even those to whom he was closest, the people he loved brought so much light to his life, Daniel thought, a series of visits that morning moved him to this acknowledgement of life, Eddy's letter, Samuel's email, J'aime's brief appearance, and he thought of those paintings of J'aime's that he'd never expected, wasn't it a miracle that J'aime, in spite of the crippling cerebral palsy that mangled his nerves and made his every movement a caricature, disfigured him, his body folded in on itself, the clutched body imposed on him, the gift of a life diminished from the start and his condition without any expectation of improvement and which would decline steadily over time, what an inexplicable wonder it was that J'aime had such talent for the arts, writing poems and film reviews and a painter too, he was such a gentle soul, though he lost all trace of that gentleness when he was painting and Daniel congratulated him for that, his fury was justified, yes, thought Daniel, it was legitimate, and quite like the other fury every bit as conspicuous in the rivers of colour of the painter Jean-Michel Basquiat, dead at twenty-seven of a heroin overdose, but no doubt the museums of New York would not be clamouring for J'aime's paintings as they had done for the works of Basquiat, so sought after and praised, J'aime, modest as ever, said he was a local painter who could only exhibit in cinemas, or would he be discovered like the sensational Black painter, both of them children of such strenuous anger, there was a photograph in a magazine that showed Basquiat at the height of his glory a few years before his death, barefoot in front of a wall on which his giant paintings of rabid animals with their fangs out were displayed, his feet were bare but he was wearing an Armani suit stained with the colours of his paintings, how beautiful he looked, how provocative, like J'aime, whose eyes gleamed with intelligence, J'aime who was devoid of malice but incapable of controlling the movements of a body gone awry, his gaze communicated such self-discipline, shouldn't Daniel have been grateful that despite the thick corset harrying J'aime's true and relinquished body and its movements all day he came to visit Daniel that morning in June, that he'd invited him to come see his paintings, those existential gifts would come back to him, thought Daniel, never washing away the sadness of Augustino's absence, Augustino, who was ever farther away, out of reach, Daniel had no idea when he would be back, tomorrow, or never, wasn't it better, within limits, to anticipate the worst, reflected Daniel, and Fleur, even if he suppressed the thought, had been so moved by the round face of Kim's child, the round cheeks, by the sincerity shining in the child's eyes, he could never forget that the child could have been his, now the nomads Rafael and Kim had a roof over their heads, they lived in a loft, though Rafael's business was as illegal as ever, he was a con man, though with all that money he could buy a sailboat, go away, Rafael and Kim and Rafael's children, out to sea, where Rafael like a pirate would continue his swindles, and Pearl Saved from the Waters would come of age unattached, Fleur thought, a wild girl who could do anything she liked, or at least until a coast guard ship turned its gun on them, no, it would never be like that, the guru Rafael was a skilful provider, that much was certain, he had always evaded the law, and Pearl Saved from the Waters would never suffer as a result of his trade, she would suffer no harm, Fleur thought, and Kim would protect her child, Kim was a fierce mother, a wolf mother, but Fleur's life was now devoted to his music and he would never see them again, neither Kim nor Jérôme the African, who was cursed, a perpetual wanderer, nor Brilliant nor Martha, his mother, nor that priest with whom she helped the refugees, Alfonso, he would never see any of them, Europe, the whole world was his island, his mother wrote him that she regretted his birth, Fleur, her son, she regretted her devotion to him long ago, traitor, all the maternal tenderness leached from her heart, she wrote to her son, you, cruel exile, you've betrayed your mother and your friends, she refused to accept any help from him, no money, even if her altruism, her work with refugees, had bankrupted her, she would have preferred Fleur had never come into the world, Fleur thought she would regret her words right away, Fleur chided himself for his silence, but that was his destiny, would it even have been possible for him to have acted any differently, he mused, he would never see them again and not without some anguish, which he stoically stifled, he kept silent, music, music, from my infancy should I not have lived only for music, like Clara, music has made me a nomad too, and destitute, but is it too late, this meandering journey along the beach, among the cardboard boxes in the streets, at the foot of buildings, his world smelled like Kim's hair, he had buried his face in it so many times, the drums of Jérôme the African sounding in the wind, they were small animals huddled together with their dogs, Damien and Max, in the haze and the cold, in winter when the ocean waves seem to crash right against them, in the night when they were so alone, wrapped in a blanket on Old Salt's boat, Old Salt who would be attacked by thugs, killed, he'd loved Kim as if she were his own daughter, and for a long, long time Kim couldn't leave the ship, she was nursing her child, it was so lonely for Kim, and Pearl Saved from the Waters, and Martha, his mother, she used to tell everyone that her son had no feelings, that he was a traitor, and Fleur couldn't stop thinking about them, even when he didn't want to, even during the concerts in Geneva and in Rome when Claudio was conducting his *New Symphony*, my god, how he would finally manage to cut himself off, they'd be on their way to Munich soon, Claudio said in the morning over a cup of cold coffee, at noon they'd have a quick lunch in Rome on the terrace of a restaurant Claudio liked because it was frequented by lots of musicians, everything always went very fast with Claudio, Fleur was dizzy from the insistent morning light streaming through the trees and all the people walking, was there a stain on his white shirt or on his faded blue jeans, did it show in the sun, Fleur wondered, and meanwhile Claudio was always so impeccably dressed, just like when he went out in the evening, a silk scarf around his neck and his straight, longish hair framing his angular face, Claudio's wife Anietta, who was a violinist in the orchestra, used to say of Claudio that he was so distracted when he went to Mass with his children he would wander off on his way home, or was it on his way to the church, was this absent-mindedness of his attractive, Fleur wondered, was it deliberate, Fleur was irritated that Claudio actually went to church, that he stayed true to a contemptible religion that guided him without ever freeing him, or could he hear the voice of Wrath mocking the Catholics so eager to buy into the idolatry of a great, absent God, I was thinking of you a few days ago, Claudio said to Fleur, my orchestra played with a young Russian prodigy who had recently won the Tchaikovsky and Rubinstein competitions, from the age of nine this boy lived to memorize music in his head no matter where he went, at school, on the train, on the metro, his piano scores, his musician parents had left their village to live closer to Moscow, twenty-five is a critical age for a prodigy, Claudio used to say, virtuosity must surpass itself to be fully realized, isn't it too much pressure, all those concerts, a pianist never stops, one hundred and thirty concerts a year, isn't that too demanding, but Chris, the young musician, he never stops touring, he never stops working, building up his technique, he makes video recordings of himself playing to analyze his weak points, he works painstakingly on what he calls the transition from fortissimo to whisper, to breath, but curiously Chris says you have to play all instruments without passion, he thinks passion is intrusive, a bother, Fleur listened to Claudio and noticed he wasn't smoking, it had been a while, now he only smoked in the street and only briefly, but passion is the source of music Fleur wanted to say but didn't say anything, you need to be impassioned otherwise it's not music, what nonsense was he about to utter, he was a musician by instinct, an indigent prodigy, so uncultured compared to Claudio, who knew so much, Claudio looked young but when he was conducting, Fleur thought, he seemed older, he tied his hair back with an elastic that blended into his hair, the velour elastic was perhaps a bit vain, and he conducted with such drama, his arms raised, his expression intense, up on the podium Claudio would give in to some romantic idea of himself, though he never did this in his daily life, he was a religious man and an austere man, Fleur thought, and Claudio asked Fleur a question, calling him by his given name, Andrew, so Andrew, he said, are you ready to face the concert hall in Munich with me, you know, dear friend, I respect you only when you stop doubting your immense talent, but I can see you're a bit afraid, and as Claudio spoke with the confidence that came to him so naturally, his hair flying in his face, Fleur caught a glimpse of the newspaper, it was sitting between them on the table, Claudio had bought it in the morning but he hadn't yet seen the headlines that caught Fleur's eye, at this very moment the day before, just before noon, there had been a massacre in a high school in a small quiet town in Germany, like the Columbine shooting in the States, now Germany had its Columbine, high school students and their teachers murdered, killed by a student who had been expelled from the school for aggressive behaviour, the paper said, and Fleur thought, no, it can't go on like this any longer, we have to take a stand, I'll write an opera describing these victims, their inconsolable parents, there are no words, there is no embrace, Fleur had gone pale, he wasn't listening to Claudio any more, a high school girl said they were my friends, my classmates, he killed them, when you see blood on television, you don't think it's real, but here, at our high school, it was, the murderer wore a mask, we didn't see it coming, he threw open the door to our classroom and he shot our teacher, there was blood everywhere, it wasn't like on TV, it was real, and just like the carnage at Columbine, the massacre stopped at noon when the masked killer turned his gun on himself, was this Hiroshima all over again, the girls whose limbs the explosion had plastered to the blackened trees in an instant, charred, we could write how familiar these tragedies were, the man in the mask dressed in black killing methodically, methodically, the paper said, going from one classroom to the next, first the teachers and then the students, in the quiet town of Erfurt, Germany, a small town that had kept something of the Middle Ages, a quiet town in Eastern Germany, now, Fleur thought, the blood of high school students, schoolchildren, shed in parallel from one country to another, one city to another, perhaps the murderer had stopped and turned the weapon against himself when he found himself standing in front of an empty classroom, until the piano emitted barely a murmur, a breath, Fleur thought, the music dying out gently beneath the fingers of the virtuoso pianist, Chris, like the breath of the children, the children of the city of Erfurt, the children of Hiroshima, a journalist asked do we need to turn our schools into fortresses, is that what we have to do, and Claudio drank his coffee and said even if Chris denies that there's any passion when he's at the piano, I would say he plays in a fiery way, it's incandescent, he's more sensitive than he admits, and yet shouldn't extraordinarily gifted musicians, whether they're composers or concert musicians, shouldn't they be wary of mental imbalance, of madness, of some pathological disorder that is the inevitable companion of the depression that typically undermines them, I think of George Gershwin writing his opera *Porgy and Bess*, or Tchaikovsky and his first piano concerto, so full of despair, Gershwin composed his opera while he was dying of a brain tumour, that's where the depths of his melancholy came from, and as he finished his coffee Claudio folded the newspaper back into his leather briefcase, rummaging in the pocket of his suit with one hand to find a cigarette, and in no time they were back on the street and heading for the restaurant Claudio had chosen, so what do you think, Andrew, about your *New Symphony* in Munich, you didn't say, Claudio was talking to Fleur but Fleur was distracted and the words were lost in the morning din of the street, Claudio answered his cell phone, yes, he would be there, yes, he was telling his daughter he'd be at the cello lesson, he'd drive her there at five o'clock, he was so sweet with her, positively gushing love, she was only seven years old, she was learning to sing with her sister too, his children would remain little girls for some time yet, he said to Fleur, they wouldn't be pushed to grow up too fast, for some time yet there would be nothing for them but the beauty of music, they weren't allowed to watch television more than once a week, that was it, and the parents decided what they were allowed to watch, my children must be able to sleep well and without nightmares, Claudio's phone started to ring, he jotted down his business appointments, too bad he was so busy, he told Fleur, and, taking Fleur's arm, added, come to our rehearsal tonight, you will hear the moment of silence before the flute comes in and what you describe as the cooing of a dove, complete stillness, a silence at noon that brings to mind the voice of the cuckoo in Vivaldi's *Four Seasons* though with an almost mocking difference, all at once everything comes to a standstill and the cuckoo sings, it's spring, life, and for us believers listening to the music it would be a form of resurrection, yes, but sometimes I think I am wrong to believe that resurrection is the most beautiful of promises, even in our world, Fleur listened to Claudio as he breathed in the summer air, and Claudio had put away the paper, sparing Fleur from having to see it, the morning news tucked amid the scores and documents in his leather briefcase, Claudio wouldn't hear of the massacre, so similar to the one at Columbine, until the following day on the train to Munich, silenced by the news until shortly before the hour of the concert when he asked Fleur, almost defiantly, tell me, Andrew, what would we do without faith, what would become of us if God didn't exist, don't you see that we have to believe, don't all men need hope, didn't you yourself leave the song of the dove in your symphony, in which everything seems falsely cacophonous and discordant, a song that is a signal of happiness, of deliverance, your musical ear managed to catch it, and Fleur had thought but did not say, Claudio, don't bow down to some imperious religion that treats you like a drudge, don't align yourself with its lies and hypocrisy, why are you so blind to the swindle, but it was Wrath's voice Fleur now heard behind him, as if the old man, with his fetid breath and in all his decay, had been at his side the whole time, in the same mangy coat he'd been wearing when Fleur met him on the banks of the Seine after a concert in Paris, shivering in his coat, the old man said, I have several things to teach you about the world of the wretched I belonged to for a long time, listen to me, don't run away from me, this was before I became an outcast, before I lived under the bridge, I saw them, a cluster of cardinals around a red carpet, the hair below their red caps had gone white, they were ancient, this was just a few years ago, and a very old pope sat curled up in his white chair with his head bowed, the Pope was said to be a good and honest man and he would be elevated to sainthood by the church soon after, but on that day he was simply an ailing, beggarly chief perusing newspaper articles with his cardinals, they had to admit it, the outrage had crossed the ocean, articles vehemently condemning them, articles with unspeakable allegations they read incredulously because none of these disturbing allegations could be true, they were all thinking it, one of them was already challenging the accusation, whether it was true of the priest named, I remember that to avoid a scandal we sent him on a mission to Peru, we don't like this sort of scandal, yes, we had heard about the abuse but never believed it was true, it goes without saying, there was talk of three hundred cases of abuse, but it's just not realistic, the priest lived in a small village and was in charge of the souls there, but three hundred cases of abuse, certainly not, another priest had been denounced in a parish in Chicago, we sent him on a mission to Chile, gentlemen, these accusations coming to light, from Peru, from Guatemala, they're extremely disturbing and offensive, they must not be exposed further, these voices must be silenced, we mustn't hear about this any longer, how can this be happening when we send these unfortunates farther and farther away, from one country to another, we who aspire only to silence, to piety before the gaze of an infinite God, gentlemen, I am calling for silence, suppression and silence, these are international cases that will involve lawyers and legal experts against us, we must keep silent, isn't that our motto, it's sensible, when we send them to Third World countries, whatever they do we don't hear much about it, these are countries of oblivion, repudiated in our eyes and in the eyes of others, we cannot take into consideration all the children who say they've been abused, we cannot, their allegations, these allegations by the victims' lawyers, they're from so long ago that we don't even remember, and these articles make us out to be predators, predators, I order you, gentlemen, protect our cardinals, and our bishops, against whom there have also been damning allegations, not to name anybody, no, no, this meeting was taking place in Vatican City, there is another solution, the cardinal said from below his red cap, we can appease them by offering them a certain amount of money, not excessive of course, it could conclude a pact of silence, I confess that I find it hard to believe that one of our cardinals was arrested and imprisoned in Brazil recently without our knowledge, no one can be judged without our permission, gentlemen, be vigilant, do not allow this, in our higher ranks this cannot be allowed, it cannot be tolerated, see to it this does not happen again, and the very old pope, the holy man, consented to the protection of the bishops, the cardinals, but woe unto him who should cause a scandal, he said, how could someone sexually assault children, the little ones, his flock, the Lord's lambs, how could someone do this, it was as if the children's throats had been slit, the innocent sheep, he was so weakened by old age he wanted to weep, had he been younger he would have recommended sanctions, yes, he would have been merciless, but he was worn out, diminished by so many duties, no one seemed to understand him, they said he was good but he felt a troubling cravenness, it was because he had no strength left, it was time for God to come and pluck him like an overripe fruit, there was twilight even for saints, yes, he felt himself unworthy of holiness, it existed even for him, the thick night was closing in, and where was God, where was the city of heaven with its golden light, he saw before him this assembly of old men, each one more obtuse than the next, some of them were deaf, others had fallen asleep reading the articles condemning them, may God have mercy on them, the old pope suffered from acute rheumatism, what a dark night it was, he thought, yes it was, may God forgive him his silence, he no longer had the strength, this culture of secrecy, of silence, it had gone on too long, these tragic errors as we so hypocritically call them, the aged pope longed for sleep, for tranquility, for there to be nobody around him, in the past he would have acted differently, the cardinal has found a solution, he heard one of them say, yes, compensation of eighteen million dollars, we need to mention one particular accusation, a violation, according to this article that's so critical of our Holy Church, of the trust of a young boy by the accused priest in question, let us call him Paul, his victim, let us call the child Robert, the article goes on spitefully, the young boy later committed suicide and his family in Connecticut is asking for money, but I would point out that the suicide of a boy who was unstable at school and who benefited from the teaching of the priest Paul may have had nothing to do with the accused priest, rather, he may have been the victim of his own instability, why accuse the priests, consecrated in their doctrine, I doubt the veracity of this accusation, the cardinal said with the utmost arrogance, these articles, he went on, also accuse our priests of having raped children during prayer retreats every year before Easter, I assure you, gentlemen, it is insidious, and on this matter also I urge your complicity, because these accusations are false and are made against us in order to diminish the holiness of our church and its spiritual influence in the world, I assure you, gentlemen, I assure you, this drivel was painful for the very old pope to hear, sitting in his white armchair he'd stopped listening, God had abandoned him to this shipwreck, he thought, he was losing his faculties, and his spirit looked upon his lambs, his bloodied sheep passing before him, and he thought, oh, how long the night would be, yes, God had forsaken him, he was too simple a man for holiness, the Pope thought, and that's how it was, the consistory, just like I'm telling you, Wrath said to Fleur, I was there, I saw it all, it was in Vatican City, I was getting ready to leave for Asia myself, on the pretext of an evangelical mission, I was among the accused being protected by these men of God who love neither God nor men, but my faults had been concealed, they weren't preoccupied with what they used to call my waywardness with the altar boys, and at the mission in Asia I wouldn't make any more noise, at least not until someone came to persecute me, to throw me into the street, I'd met Tai, in a way I bought him from his parents, Tai, who betrayed me even though I gave him everything, I had adopted him as a son when I was covered in riches, in the wealth of the Church, first we left Asia for Europe, that's where we went first, I would always be on the run, until I was betrayed and my infamous mother, the Church, threw me out, and here I am now living hidden among the most wretched of men, here I am, said Wrath to Fleur, who was always alert to Wrath's voice, who could never put him out of his mind, and across from him in the train car, Claudio was lost in his own thoughts, and from behind the curtain of his hair he said out of nowhere to Fleur, removing the earphones from his ears, I was listening to Mahler's

Kindertotenlieder, his *Songs on the Death of Children*, I have
to find a way to conduct that piece in a more balanced
manner, we conductors tend to put too much exuberance
into it and not enough reflection, no doubt Mahler, who
was one of the greatest conductors, no doubt he was the
only one who knew how to conduct it contemplatively, in
order to meditate on the injustice of death, which when it
strikes children is a form of murder, I am learning, I still
have a lot to learn from these great works, *The Song of the
Earth*, *Songs on the Death of Children*, Claudio's delicate
fingers seemed to be leading an imaginary orchestra, his
voice shaping almost atonal whispers, spoken internally,
Kindertotenlieder, Kindertoten, his reflection is so rigorous,
Claudio said, as his fingers continued to draw in the air,
there is so much to learn, he repeated, and how can we
not be furious to think that Mahler's compositions were
banned throughout the Nazi Reich and in much of Europe,
suppression through silence, he said, how many works and
composers have been silenced so that today we know
nothing about them, art must overcome dictatorship and
war, Claudio went on, and art will overcome, you will be a
witness to this and I will too, you, Andrew, you know it
well, you are the artist as survivor, emancipated from your
prison, from the silence that oppressed you, am I not right
to believe in this promise of the resurrection, even in our
world where there is so much suffering, suffering we can
name and other torments that are unspeakable, hellish, am
I not a little bit right, yes, you may be right, Fleur said,
avoiding Claudio's eyes and turning instead to the window
and the landscape tearing by, night and day, the Young Man
thought of him, Pastor Anna's son, and then the other man,
the son of one of the mothers he had killed, he was terrified

of running into him in the showers or in the hallway leading
to the execution chamber, he worried about his still-cherubic
face, which in an instant an avenger could injure and bruise,
the chastity of his face was marred by his scowl, by anger
and fear, but he had to keep up appearances, his hair layered down across his forehead, he held himself up straight
and righteously, they would continue to see him on television and in the newspapers but from that point on he would
be dressed in his ridiculous prison jumpsuit, the uniform
was a taint on his body and he was upset, distressed, but
not his face, please, let his face be spared, let none of these
monstrous inmates damage him, what a humiliation this
was when all he had wanted was glory, the prison guards
believed he had submitted to his captive state when, after
he'd asked for paper and a pen, he'd written his manifesto
of hate, he no longer refused the meals passed to him
through the opening in the door, he had to feign good
behaviour, acceptance, he had to seem resigned to his fate,
he would fool them, at last he was able to write calmly on
his bed even if he always dreaded that a ghost would return,
either the son of Pastor Anna or another victim appearing
before him, would it happen in the showers or by the toilets,
his victim appearing with a knife and saying, here, this is
what you deserve, take this for your murders, you killed my
mother, his hair would be plaited or in locs like one of the
Blacks he abhorred, how he hated their smell, he thought,
they were all there in his dreams, praying at New Hope
Methodist Church, still praying in monotonous voices, saying,
God alone will judge you, we forgive you but our children
shall not forgive you, our children cry for vengeance, and
suddenly Pastor Anna walked up to him and with kindness
she said to him, it is not me who has blood on my hands,

it's you, didn't I warn you to go home to your parents, your murders will be remembered forever, is that what you wanted, alas, evil conquers humanity more than good, go back home to your parents, and the Young Man woke abruptly because the chaplain was there, right up against the bars of his cell, the chaplain was talking to him, I told you we'd meet again, I wanted to tell you that your lawyer will request life in prison when the court asks for the death penalty, you have a lot of people against you, I can't reassure you entirely though I'd like to, but you're young, it's not often that young murderers commit such serious crimes, believe me, I wish it were otherwise, but could you not express some remorse, repent a little, your attitude will work against you, I'm telling you, the judge could spare you in the sentencing if you seemed more repentant, they don't like your indifference, you seem cold, I want to die as the hero of the White Supremacist Youth, the Young Man thought, but my face will be crumpled and twitching when I'm strapped down on a bed I will refuse to lie on, I shall hold my head high like a drowning man above the water, I shall have written it in my Manifesto of Hate that I intend to die as a hero so that other white supremacists follow, young people, the very young, my sacrifice will be for them, may they listen to me, the white race is at war with the Black race and all races of colour, we lost our pride in being white when slavery was abolished and our great-grandparents gave up the principles of racial segregation, but if he was imprisoned for life the Young Man would secretly build his network online, his manifesto would be more widely known and celebrated, he knew he wasn't alone, there were countless others who had read and encouraged his campaign of hate, they were legion, but these last few days he had been banned from possessing any propaganda, he was being censored, yes, that was it, but hatred cannot be censored, the Young Man thought, and then, remembering the murderer Michael, he wondered if someone would come to get him without ever telling him the day or the time, might it be on shower day, that day he feared so much, a guard standing on the other side of the bars like the chaplain earlier today, the chaplain had said he wanted what was best and for him to confess, and the expression of the officer or the guard who came to him would also be kind, no doubt because of his youth, and the man would say to the Young Man, you get a last meal, don't hesitate to request a top-quality steak and your favourite dessert, we noticed that you like sweets, we have some delicious treats for the occasion, we'll come to you with information, the chaplain at the head of our solemn group, no matter what you think, we believe in this solemnity for inmates condemned to the ultimate punishment, we believe in it, those nights are never quite normal and we never forget them, we will stride solemnly by your side, your wrists will be bound, and some of the condemned, we've seen it happen, they physically collapse before we reach the hallway and the chamber, they faint out of fear, they go into cardiac arrest and we have to shake them to revive them, we know how agonizing it can be for them, the fear, the terror that clenches in their chest, some ask for a sleeping pill, which we have to refuse because they're required to have a clear conscience before the punishment, only then will your crimes be forgiven, that's how it will be, the Young Man thought, and would they be all behind the glass wall with the son of Pastor Anna, some saying we forgive him because we are Christian, others yelling let him be tortured, yes, would they all be there, with his parents moaning and pleading for their son to be saved, he was still their boy, they would say in the midst of the horror that he was their child, is that how his last day would go, his last hour ending at one minute past midnight as it had for the murderer Michael, is that how it would be, the Young Man wondered, and Asoka the monk had written to Lou, my dear Lou, I am back in Mongolia, and a friend from the village near the orphanage where I visit my orphans came to bring me your email message for my birthday, you can't imagine the joy I felt when I received it, you say that you've been searching for me for a long time, but you know that as a wandering monk I never stop travelling from one end of the earth to the other, I am often on the road, my lodgings are uncomfortable, I am more than forty now and the pilgrim's life is more difficult, but I continue my teachings in the company of those in the monasteries and on the road who wish for a better world, I always feel much sorrow when I visit the orphanages, these poor children left behind by the war, we must show them love because they have been abandoned, they have nothing, in Töv I am welcomed as before by the monks, and my orphans have grown up, they sang and danced for me in their costumes and I blessed them as before, but I am sorry, dearest Lou, that your father Ari is no longer publishing my magazine *The Evolution of Consciousness* on your island, why is that, dear Lou, has he lost confidence in me, in our friendship of yesteryear, well, regardless, I thank him for the happiness he gave me when he was assisting my publication, you say that Ari is interested only in his sculptures now and so I say to you that it is well and good, I should no longer impose on him in any way, dear goddaughter, I would very much like to see you again, you were so tiny when I saw you last and your parents were happy together, it was also a delight for me to see you together, you say that later, when you are eighteen, you will come to Mongolia and I believe you, in the monasteries here we take in visitors, they are getting younger and younger by the day, we ask them to respect our spiritual practice, though it's not necessary for them to pray with us, we tell them about the beauty of the universe and ask that they learn to reflect on nature and animals, every animal, even the monkeys that come up to our monasteries, we ask that our visitors accompany our prayers in silence and learn how to meditate, these very young followers from so far away, we await them in quiet meditation, and I know that one day you'll be here too, the rules for our novices are strict and incontrovertible, chastity and total obedience, the vow of chastity was the most demanding for me because I would have liked very much to be a father, but I had the happiness to meet your parents, Ingrid, Ari, during a visit to your country when Ari and I were editing *The Evolution of Consciousness* and the two of them asked me to be your godfather, this was long before their divorce and when everything was going well, as you write, but I don't want their strife or separation to sadden you, as you say, no, I don't want that, there are so many sorrows in this world, know that they still love you as much as ever, with the same fervour, every feeling on earth tends to change, we ourselves change every day and you yourself will soon be in the splendour of adolescence, so forget the sorrows that afflicted you and think of my orphans, who have never received anything like the kindnesses you've received, you must help others and forget yourself, at one time Ari believed the same thing too, you must be capable of deprivation, that's what Ari wrote to me

when we were editing the magazine together, my teachings
have taken me back to the Gal Oya Valley in Sri Lanka, and
as I described to your father once, terrorists emerged from
that valley, they killed thousands of civilians and I am always
a bit afraid when I cross the jungle, but I have to go on my
own to the soldiers' bunker to comfort them, they walk
between life and death, and in the face of so much conflict
I'm always amazed to see a tree I remember from childhood
in bloom, or the vanilla-scented orchids, their smell comes
over me and I say to myself, what a joy it is to be alive, to
be able to breathe this perfume, I think of my sister Matupali,
she's the only sister I have left and I don't know when I
will see her, my two other sisters lost their lives when the
north of Sri Lanka, my country, was destroyed, I can still
see the rows of trucks passing in front of me full of the
dead, women, children, I told myself that in memory of my
sisters I had to open a centre for education there, that was
my duty, to do so right there, and that's why I came back,
how fortunate you are, my little Lou, to be able to attend
to your studies every day, in this valley the teachers and
children go to schools that have been bombed, destroyed,
yet it is here in Mongolia that I will open a new education
centre for orphans, from beyond the grave my sisters ask
this of me, you tell me, Lou, that your father is now pros-
perous, and that this is why he denies ever wanting to live
ascetically, these words were also words he once used, but
now his sculptures sell regularly all over the world, you say,
I'm delighted with you, little Lou, but you need to learn
how to empty yourself of everything from the inside, you
also tell me that your mother, Ingrid, left your father because
he was unfaithful to her, over and over, you say, but you
need to understand, Lou, that men are made this way, the

gift of fidelity is not given to everyone, though what a disappointment it must be for you who would like to be part of a united family, I must admit that it came as a shock to me too, Ari once seemed to me such a generous, harmonious being, my dear Lou, and it's also true that men more than women change with age, I can't tell you much about that because I'm only a pilgrim, forever dressed in the same orange tunic and begging in the villages almost barefoot, as I've been doing since I was a child, I've hardly changed compared to Ari, who was offered all sorts of opportunities to develop and to change himself and every temptation of a secular life, I am a humble pilgrim monk, but what respect, even deference, I have for you, for your father who loves you, and for your mother, Ingrid, never doubt that they love you, I was so young when I was separated from my family, at sixteen I began my studies as a novice, Daddy believes in the satisfaction of all pleasures, you write, how will he recover the calm of his meditations of yesteryear, how, my dear Lou, will the tension he harbours in a life too full of disturbances be stilled, we must commit, as I taught Ari long ago, to enlightened harmony, and dear Lou, you say too that you are no longer a girl but a boy, that boys are much luckier in life, that you now dress like a boy, even at school, and that you want to be a boy like your brother Julien, I confess I don't really understand what it is you are writing to me, I look at your photograph, and it is true that you look more and more like your brother but you are a girl, not a boy, I remember you as a charming little girl, you liked athletics and hard sports but you wore dresses and you really were a girl, it must be said that you were a child then, but I never would have suspected that one day you would feel the desire to be a boy like Julien, have you spoken about this with your parents, what do they think about it, I'm not a psychologist, I have no such knowledge, I am only your godfather, a humble monk who knows only the hearts and souls of men, but I will admit to you that it may be that we are born double, born with a mind and a body, or a soul and a body, that are not necessarily compatible, the body cannot be born perfectly matched with the spirit, for then we would be another kind of creature, without anguish perhaps, and certainly very different from what we are, but here I am treading among ideas the dimensions of which elude me, you say too that you would like to change your first name, Lou, Marie-Louise, into a more masculine first name, Benjamin, how in the future could I write no longer to Lou but to Benjamin, but who is this Benjamin, I don't know him, if she is no longer my goddaughter Lou, then who is she, can you enlighten me further, perhaps I can love Benjamin as much as Lou, perhaps they are one, and out of deference, out of respect for the being that you are, I don't have to choose, I can respect both, isn't the essential thing to be good, or to be capable of goodness, and on these words, I bless you, my dear little Lou, and your daddy Ari and your mama Ingrid, signed, your loving godfather, Asoka, hey, Robbie shouted, look at the pelicans swooping over the waves, so slowly, we're a few steps away from Pelican Beach, it's almost noon and it's getting hotter and hotter, what a great day for our Angel, Robbie said to Petites Cendres, but Petites Cendres was distracted by Brilliant whirling around and Misha right behind him, against his back, I thought about what you were saying this morning, Robbie, I'll go with you and Yinn and the other girls to San Francisco for the demonstration Yinn and his friends are organizing, I'll go, because if a bad law is passed that legalizes contempt, well that means any bad law can be allowed, there'll be a whole pile of bad laws and crime after crime against us, and Robbie said I always knew you'd come with us, Petites Cendres, the whole world will support us, Yinn said so, we won't be on our own anymore and the persecution will be over, it will come to an end, Yinn says, the cruelty, but in the meantime, Victoire can't even use a public restroom without being humiliated, ostracized, or even arrested, and she's an engineer, a respectable woman, in the meantime, Robbie repeated, transgender children are being kicked out of the washrooms at school, where are they supposed to go, must they pee out in the street, yeah, where will they go, can a whole society punish innocents, Yinn is sure it will come to an end, Petites Cendres said, and you have to believe him, he never lies, Yinn believes in a positive revolution, Petites Cendres said again, you sound like you're losing your voice, Robbie said to Petites Cendres, drink some more water, your hair is all sweaty, Robbie said anxiously, maybe you have a fever, but Petites Cendres told Robbie that he'd never felt better, and anyway, Mabel said, up on a platform on Pelican Beach, the Black Ancestral Choir had begun to sing among the sublime birds, Eureka joining in songs for Angel, Angel, whom she'd spoiled and cared for so much, Eureka's soprano voice was jubilant in the gentle breeze, Robbie said, it announced to everyone that Angel was already without a doubt at the feet of Jesus, in the warm midday air the song rose from Eureka's lips to reach the luminous sky and those gathered on the sand listened, Brilliant thundered past Mabel, Petites Cendres, and Robbie, running ahead with Misha, Brilliant had met up with Lucia and Lena on the beach, hadn't he said it would be a day full of surprises, Petites Cendres saw Brilliant kneeling in front of Lucia, telling her that he wanted to marry her, can you be married on a day of mourning, Mabel asked, wouldn't that be forbidden, forbidden by whom, Robbie asked, mourning can't last, life must go on Robbie said, but Lucia is my age, Mabel said, and he's just a boy, oh don't bother them in their happiness, Robbie impatiently replied, be happy that they're happy and just think how much more convenient it will be, they'll share the same car, the same apartment in the Acacia Gardens, and they'll have Misha with them, what could be more perfect, and Brilliant has just earned his nursing degree, soon he'll be able to help Dr. Dieudonné at the clinic, there's so much to do, so many people to heal, it'll be an excellent marriage Robbie said, but Brilliant must not open the champagne before Angel's ashes are scattered in the sea, that was what he wanted, poor thing, Mabel said, and soon I'll be able to lay a very heavy weight in the ocean, there'll be a boat waiting for you at the pier, Robbie said, come, let me carry the bag for you, we're almost there, don't let Brilliant open the champagne too soon, Mabel said again, it wouldn't be respectful of Angel, Lena, his mother, said love is better than respect, love is a decent virtue too Robbie added, I can hear the voice of Reverend Stone, they're close and listening to him, Yinn and the queens and even Victoire, they're all there in their crowns and feathers and finery, Robbie said, what songs, what sweet sermons, Angel I'm sure is happy at the feet of Jesus, Mabel said, oh stop it with your religion, Robbie replied, here's Reverend Stone repeating the sermon he gave for Fatalité, yeah, wanting us to believe that God the Father is bringing His son Angel home, our treasure, bringing him back to His paradise where all misery is forgotten, what a tedious man, Robbie said, it's always the same litany, for

Herman, for Fatalité, and now for Angel, he's never very inspired, shut up, Mabel said, Reverend Stone speaks the truth, our Father in heaven is truly Angel's father and the father of us all, yes, He makes no distinction between any of us, Mabel said, lies, the whole of it, Robbie said, pure fantasy, Robbie said, I can't wait for us to raise a glass at Brilliant and Lucia's wedding, Petites Cendres said, what a perfect day to get married, Robbie said, but Petites Cendres had noticed the man with a red balloon for a head, which inflated and deflated under his straw hat as he insulted Petites Cendres and his friends, now a whole group of similar characters with masks on their faces and caps folded over their eyes was with him and shouting slurs as they made their way in a procession down to Pelican Beach, they were yelling and noisy and hostile, though Petites Cendres couldn't make out what they were saying over the sound of the waves, though the chorus of hatred was deafening and it worried him, would those men, those women, assault the Black Ancestral Choir, or Eureka, who was singing her most moving songs for Angel, would the enchantment of their voices be cut off by the foul voices of that second choir, Petites Cendres worried, why didn't Reverend Stone call them out, what a weak man he was, he was so gullible, how could he not see the hatred in that bunch, it was unfor-givable, Petites Cendres thought, but Reverend Stone, his hair pushed straight up by the wind, carried on, God was the father of us all, yes, all of us, the cruise ship has almost docked, Mabel said, the cruise ship, the luxury ship and its luxury passengers, what will become of the little boats, look, they're screaming, they're doomed and nobody is coming to help, will they have drowned by nightfall, one wave and they could sink to the bottom of the ocean, one wave, Mabel

said, ah, as you say, Petites Cendres, it's a wonderful day to
get married, they deserve it, Lucia and Brilliant, if God loves
joy and humour, He will have His fill with them, they're
cheerful and lively, their star shines bright, though I must
keep in mind that Lucia is far too old for Brilliant, crazy
Brilliant, his heart is as wide as an empire even if his empire
is almost broke, he rejects what he calls his mother's dirty
money, his mother, the mayor, the woman who used to beat
him, well that's how it goes, all those men, those women
who've come over from Africa on rafts, their skin is the
same colour as mine, can it be true that tonight they may
end up lying at the bottom of the ocean, they cry and they
wail and I must ask the Lord why this is His will, why, I
have no answer in my prayers, Mabel thought, Jerry's beak
was digging through her hair, Jerry, darling, Mabel said,
aside from my grandchildren, and I have many, you're the
one I love the most, you and I are alone in the world, Merlin
has left us, he's buried at the foot of the rosebush, Merlin
is no more, he was killed by a stone thrown by a pernicious
child, oh Merlin, and Mabel said to Jerry, when will they
stop murdering our people, Mama, our people, repeated
Jerry, Mama, where is Merlin, and Claudio was in the train
car to Munich, he had almost fallen asleep in his seat listening to the music on his headphones, and Fleur heard Wrath's
voice, much as he fought it he could never forget it, that
voice emerging from unattainable depths from which no
light seeped forth, though who knows if his might not be
the voice of a desperate prophet dehumanized by misery,
debased to the point of inhumanity, because he said it himself, he was an excommunicated priest living among people
infested with vices, with the most wretched, under bridges,
in the mud, with the rats, though with the science of

misfortune, Wrath's voice said, we learn everything, and what I see, my dear Fleur, is that in Rome, the city you love, with your concerts and your earthly delights, with your friend, the believer Claudio, who conducts your *New Symphony* so well, so masterfully, travelling from one European city to the next, what I see, Wrath said in Fleur's ear, is that you don't understand that in a very short time those in the caravans and camps I saw in Ireland, in those horse-drawn carts where a young red-haired queen, a queen in rags now, her kingdom defeated, a homeless pauper, yelling that she must be allowed to pass with her charge, yelling that from now on the world will be ours, it will be theirs, it will belong to refugees without passports, whether they arrive by the millions in those same horse-drawn carts or on foot, their bags on their backs, beware, she said, beware of your sumptuous avenues, your basilicas and your cathedrals, citizens of Rome and all the cities of Europe, we are coming, your city will be ours, we shall spread our rags and our sorrows and squander your unassailable goods, oh we shall, and Wrath's voice went silent, he was holding back, and Claudio stirred gently and asked, tell me, Andrew, how will your opera start, can you tell me what you're hearing, what you see, in the beginning, Fleur replied at once, inspired by his new vision and touched that Claudio was interested, at the beginning you hear sounds like a very calm quartet, perhaps a voice, a song, because the class is focused on their studies, on knowledge, and then I hear a cello, a flute, a clarinet, the students are concentrating and everything is calm, and as he continued the description of his opera, Fleur heard only the serene music he would compose, although smouldering beneath the hush, tragedy rumbled, but for as long as he spoke to Claudio, listening so attentively, Fleur believed

Wrath's voice had faded, Wrath had fallen silent, as if he had decided to entrust Fleur to the breath of music, hadn't he told Fleur once that only music would save him, hadn't he said that, and Daniel got a message from Mai telling him that they were back at the marina, Samuel's boat would be moored shortly, Mai and Mélanie had seen the sea turtles, the students at the veterinary college had worked wonders with the injured creatures, all of them returned to their home in the ocean, all of them, Mai wrote, and seated at his office desk, Daniel was writing the story of the Young Man, the murderous hero of a June morning awaiting his sentence behind bars, crouched on his bed, the Young Man was writing his manifesto and biting his nails, he was hungry, he was thirsty, but the only thing he could think of was his manifesto, because who was to say if today was the day that the guard might approach, the group of four intruding upon the silence of his cell and saying today's the day, it's time, we must prepare you for the chamber, the chamber at the end of death row, and then what would he say, probably, like Michael the convict, no, he wasn't ready, no, not today, he had a duty, he had to write his manifesto of hate, a manifesto without end, tomorrow he would be the youngest hero of the White Supremacist Youth, and Mai listened to the song of the waves and thought, how sweet was our crossing, *Southern Light*, light of the south.

About the Author

Photo by Jill Glessing

MARIE-CLAIRE BLAIS is the internationally revered author of more than twenty-five books, many of which have been published around the world. In addition to the Governor General's Literary Award for Fiction, which she has won four times, Blais has been awarded the Gilles-Corbeil Prize, the Médicis Prize, the Molson Prize, and Guggenheim Fellowships. She divides her time between Key West, Florida, and Quebec.

KATIA GRUBISIC is a Canadian writer, editor, and translator living in Montreal. Her work has appeared in the *Malahat Review*, *Grain*, and *Prairie Fire*, and she served as the editor-in-chief of *Arc Poetry Magazine*. Her collection of poems *What if red ran out* won the Gerald Lampert Memorial Award for best first book of poetry and was shortlisted for the A. M. Klein Prize for Poetry. *Brothers*, her translation of David Clerson's *Frères*, was a finalist for the Governor General's Literary Award.